WOLF'S DUTY

BOOK 2 OF THE SHADOW MOON SHIFTERS SERIES

AVA BLAKE

This is a work of fiction. The characters and events described herein are imaginary and are not intended to refer to specific places or to living persons alive or dead. All rights reserved. No part of this publication may be reproduced, distributed, or transmitted in any form or by any means, including photocopying, recording, or other electronic or mechanical methods without the prior written permission of the publisher except for brief quotations embodied in critical reviews.

Cover by TheBookBrander.com

Copyright © 2023 by Ava Blake

All rights reserved.

4

CHAPTER ONE

I groaned as Glenn, Hunter, and Blade argued for the thousandth time about who had to do what. I was surprised when they butted heads more about what chore went to which man than about who got to take the bedroom beside mine. Guys, am I right?

Tired of their bickering, I grabbed my planner and settled into grandma's office, content to leave them to their own devices while I got some work done.

I opened the planner and frowned, glancing at the current date. July 21st. How did time move so quickly? It was only early May when I first moved to Wolf Lake, Colorado. My grandma, Eustice Cummings, died of dementia and left me a large house with a chunk of land, a fat bank account, and a book and tea shop. Oh, and a crazy ass role as some sort of supernatural mediator.

I was still coming to terms with that last part. Before coming to Wolf Lake, I was just your run-of-the-mill unwanted child. Abused and unwanted by a mother who was more interested in booze and pills than ensuring I had a proper upbringing. Despite Mom's best attempts to keep me away, Grandma and I found a way to connect. She offered me a lifeline that I wish I had jumped on before she wasn't around anymore.

Now here I was, a business owner, a supernatural mediator of some sort, a freaking wolf shifter, and totally overwhelmed by life. Did I mention that I have three hotter-than-hell-fated mates? And that I'm supposed to stop some sort of evil shadow creatures that are stealing people's souls? Yeah, I was still trying to come to terms with all of that, too.

I almost ran away, but when Hunter, one of those three supposed mates, was injured by those damn shadow monsters, it was bind our souls together or let him die. That made me realize that I really, really didn't want anything bad to happen to him, or the other two.

Which is how we got here, with three sexy men bickering upstairs about who gets to cook and clean while I try to get something resembling work done.

When another door slammed, I growled and slammed my book shut, stomping out to the main hall to put a stop to their nonsense.

"Dammit Hunter! Glenn! Blade! You stop fighting this instant, you hear me? We are a fucking mate circle, whether you assholes like it or not! I expect you to at least be civil when I'm home. Now get your asses downstairs and eat your fucking lunch that I prepared."

The three men appeared at the top of the stairs, contrite looks on Blade and Hunter's faces, but a mischievous grin on Glenn's. Of course the sweet one would be the problem child.

I tried not to smirk at the sight of Hunter, his sleeves rolled up and bright pink cleaning gloves on his hands. It was a shock, considering his whole persona reminded me of super goth, a la Bam Margera and the age of Slipknot.

Glenn, bless his silly heart, was holding a broom, which he decided to use to swat Hunter in the ass as he stomped downstairs. Hunter glared back at the Moon Walker alpha, his lip curling in a sneer.

"Behave, Glenn."

He held his hands up in surrender while Blade shook his head, clearly annoyed at the man's antics. Blade was probably the most stoic of my mates, all brooding intensity and sharp as a whip mind. But still a troublemaker like the other two.

Each man was an alpha, inheriting the leadership position from their parents. Unfortunately, alphas of rival packs didn't usually get along that well, so sharing one mate had been an issue at first. It still was, to be honest. While they would rather share than have no mate at all, it wasn't in their nature to cede to another male, especially a rival alpha.

Why did I suggest moving in together, again? I rubbed a hand down my face and stalked into the kitchen, arms crossed and glaring at the stubborn men as they filed in and took their places.

"Thanks for lunch, Everly," Glenn said, still sporting that grin.

"Upstairs has been scrubbed clean, including the guest bathroom," Hunter muttered, biting into his roast beef sandwich.

Blade just rolled his eyes and ate in silence, avoiding eye contact with anyone.

Once the plates were emptied and placed into the dishwasher, I cleared my throat, looking pointedly at the three men. Hunter looked uncomfortable while Glenn looked amused, and Blade bored. Obediently, they retook their seats, watching me curiously.

"We clearly need to lay some ground rules, or I'm going to be dealing with this incessant bickering forever."

Hunter opened his mouth to no doubt make some sarcastic retort, but stopped when I held my hand up.

"I don't want to hear it. We're mates, all of us. Yes, you're all fated to me, but that means you're linked, too. You need to get along. I know it's not going to be an immediate thing, but you need to work on it. Work together, be civil. We'll start by having dinner together at least once a week. I'd prefer nightly, but I get that you each have duties to attend to, with your businesses and your packs."

"Fair enough," Hunter said, shocking me.

I eyed him closely for a moment, waiting for the other shoe to drop, before shrugging and continuing.

"I need help learning the ropes, and hopefully you can all spare the time to work on that while we get to know one another. I realize we were forced to jump into things quickly, but I don't regret it. I only regret not getting started learning what I needed sooner."

"Of course. We'll continue your lessons for as long as you need, Everly." Blade's soft words didn't surprise me, but Glenn and Hunter's emphatic agreement did.

"Good, now that's dealt with..."

"We should set date nights," Glenn interrupted me.

I swallowed nervously. I did need to get to know them better, but now that I was faced with that, I found myself more nervous than expected.

"Glenn is right," Hunter agreed.

"How about we do dinner every week, the lot of us together. Then we do date night one-on-one three other days and three days for whatever," Blade asked, and I felt his gaze raking over me, assessing my reaction.

I was glad that he took the lead, because I didn't want to fight with them about how to divvy up my time. I knew some of this tension was down to me initiating the mate bond with Hunter and not with them, and though they understood why, it didn't make it any easier on them. I needed to spend time with them—together and individually—if we were going to make this work.

"That sounds good. Do you have specific nights where you need to focus on pack duties?"

"Our pack runs are Mondays," Hunter said.

"Yeah, Moon Walker usually does pack events on Wednesdays," Glenn said with a shrug.

"Ghost Dancer runs are Sundays. So that means everyone is available for group time on Tuesdays, Thursdays, Fridays, or Saturdays."

"Why don't we plan date nights for the nights that everyone is available, so Everly can join pack events if she wants."

"Fair point, Glenn. How do you feel about that, Everly?"

"Sounds fine, but is it fair for one person to always have a weekend when the others are weekdays?"

"I don't mind," Hunter shrugged.

"Same." Glenn agreed.

Blade nodded and grabbed the large calendar that I had on the fridge.

"Let's agree to mark any important events, pack events, and date nights on here so everyone can see them. Who wants Saturdays?"

Glenn raised his hand, and Blade marked his name on the calendar across each Saturday.

"Hunter? Tuesday or Thursday?"

"Don't care, as long as I get to spend time with my mate."

Blade grunted and marked Hunter down on Thursdays, and himself on Tuesdays. He made a line through Fridays that said, 'Circle Family Night,' and then marked each pack name down on their respective nights.

"You don't *have* to join us for pack events or runs, but by having it marked on the calendar, you'll have the knowledge of when and where."

He passed the calendar around, letting each man fill out the details for their pack meetings for the rest of the month before returning it to the fridge. I watched them as they worked, pleasantly surprised to find them working together without any bickering or posturing. Maybe this whole mate circle thing really would work.

"Now, about that argument with chores. You're right, Hunter, that I shouldn't have to clean up after everyone just because I'm a woman, and I sure as hell don't plan to. We'll divide chores fairly. Everyone deals with their own personal spaces, and I'll make a chore schedule while I'm at the shop today so there's no bickering about who has to do what. I'll post it on the fridge by the calendar."

"Fair enough. I'm happy to do any maintenance as well, since it's literally my job."

"Thank you, Hunter. I'll keep that in mind. Now, did everyone have enough to eat?"

"Yep."

"Sure did."

"Thanks for lunch, Everly."

"Did you need to go to the shop today?" Blade asked with a frown, glancing at his watch.

"No, I took the day off to supervise you guys in the move… I had a feeling that we'd need to have a conversation like this."

They all had the decency to look contrite, but none of them apologized. I rolled my eyes and huffed out a breath.

As I moved to stand, Blade's phone rang. He glanced at the screen with a frown, gesturing for me to wait while he answered.

"Alpha Aspen speaking."

I strained to hear, frustrated by my lack of control over my wolf senses. Hunter was working on teaching me how to channel my wolf when in human form, but with everything that had happened recently, it was pushed to the backburner.

"Is that so?" Blade said, his frown deepening.

Hunter sucked in a sharp breath and Glenn growled a little, making my eyebrows shoot up in surprise. Glenn was the most laid back of my mates, so for him to have such a polarizing reaction to the phone call, something must be seriously wrong.

"Of course, I understand. We will all be there. Will you be informing the other alphas?"

Anger flashed in Blade's eyes at whatever the other person said. I gnawed at my lip, worry building up in my stomach as he clenched the phone tighter.

"Will you at least be informing her?"

His face pinched.

"Of course I'm capable of doing your job for you. Rest assured that the Wolf Lake council will be present."

He hung the phone up and began cursing.

"Stupid fucking Giovanni. He always pulls shit like this." Blade's eyes flashed as he clenched his fist around the phone, visibly restraining himself from throwing it.

I waited a moment for the men to calm down before glancing at Glenn, whose face was pulled tight. I'd never seen any of them this angry.

"What was that about?"

"That," Hunter growled, "was some upstart on the council trying to rile us up."

"I don't understand. What council?"

Blade blew out a long breath, melting in his chair and dropping his face into his hands.

"The council is the governing body of our world. There are two councils, one of Elders from each race, and one of Balance Keepers from each Ley Region."

I paled at his words. He once referred to my position as Watcher as a balance keeper. Did that mean that I was supposed to be on this council? I didn't even know my duties yet.

"They're calling a Summit because of the increase in Oberon attacks," Blade said miserably.

"Oh. That's good, isn't it? We could use some help."

Blade groaned and shook his head, letting Hunter take over while he had a mini meltdown.

"The Watcher position traditionally kept the attacks under control. Giovanni, the man who just called Blade, has insinuated that you can't be trusted as Watcher since the attacks have increased in your presence. He's trying to blame the increase on you and wants you punished accordingly."

My mouth dropped open in shock at those words, rage filling me. I didn't even know about this world until a few weeks ago, how could I possibly stop the epidemic of the Oberon with no training?

"What the fuck? What kind of punishment?"

Blade growled, his eyes flashing as he looked up at me.

"You won't be punished."

"What. Kind. Of. Punishment?" I demanded through gritted teeth.

It was Glenn who answered.

"Traditionally, they'd strip you of your position and bind any powers."

"Bind any powers. What does that even mean?"

The men shared a loaded look that made my stomach sink even further.

"They would bind your wolf. You'd be human again."

"Wait. But Ghost Wolf said that I'd die if she wasn't awoken...Doesn't that mean putting her back to sleep would kill me?"

"Yes."

"They want to give me a death sentence. For something beyond my control."

"Basically."

"We won't let that happen, Everly," Blade ground out.

Glenn and Hunter, for once in agreement with Blade, nodded.

"Fuck." I raked my hand through my hair. "How do we stop this? Can we just not go?"

"No. We'll teach you everything we can before then. The summit is September 1st, so we have time to prepare. I'll have the packs work together to prepare a defense. You won't deal with this alone, Everly, I promise." He glanced at the other two. "*We* promise."

They nodded their agreement, fury burning in their eyes.

"Alright, Blade, I trust you. I trust all of you."

We settled down to make another rigorous training schedule. Hunter, thankfully, didn't insist on sunrise physical training, but opted instead for seven a.m. five days a week, which was practically as bad, as far as I was concerned. Blade claimed my lunch hour three days a week and three hours of my Sunday mornings, while Glenn opted for two hours in the evening four days a week to work on my magic.

Surviving the council was one thing, but surviving the guys' attempts to save me was looking like another entirely.

CHAPTER TWO

Training started at the slightly less ridiculous hour of seven a.m., rather than the five a.m. rude awakenings Hunter had subjected me to previously. Even so, I was absolutely exhausted when he gently shook me awake at half past six.

"This is serious, Everly, no slacking off."

"I'm coming, I'm coming. Do I at least get breakfast?"

"If you get downstairs before we need to start."

I grumbled the whole way, but was downstairs within ten minutes, dressed and ready to get on with the torture. Much to my surprise, Glenn and Blade were already seated at the dining table, serving me a plate of eggs, bacon, and French toast. Of course, if this is how they were going to feed me before these torture sessions, then maybe I could actually get behind them for more than just survival.

I scarfed down the food in record time before grabbing a water bottle and rushing outside to join Hunter, who was already stretching by the time I stopped in front of him.

"Stretch out, we're going over the forms I showed you first."

"Right. So nothing new today?"

"Not today, but that doesn't make it any less important. Limber up."

"Yes, sir," I said with a salute, making Hunter smirk.

Stretching was one of the few things that I didn't need help with, ever since I had started yoga at Camille's suggestion. She said that the meditation of yoga helped you to connect with your wolf. So far, the advice seemed like bullshit, but I couldn't deny that I was much less jumpy and more in control of my emotions than I had been before I began the practice.

Hunter let me stretch for about ten minutes before clapping and pointing to the grass before him.

Obediently, I hopped to my feet and ran to a stop before him. We spent the next two hours moving through the various combat forms he had been teaching me prior to our new training schedule. I was pleasantly surprised to find that I remembered nearly everything, falling into stances as if I'd been performing the motions my whole life. Clearly, my muscle memory was better than my mind's memory.

By the time we finished, Hunter grunting his approval, I was coated with a layer of sweat.

"Same time tomorrow, little mate."

I groaned but kissed his cheek before dodging out of the way when he growled and reached for me.

"I'm all sweaty, Hunter."

He chuckled and stalked me as I raced inside, intent on getting clean before I needed to head into the bookshop at ten. I glanced at the clock on my nightstand as I grabbed clothes.

"Quarter after nine. Good, I can take a quick shower before heading in."

The sound of Hunter's chuckle from the doorway startled me, making me swirl around, clutching at my chest.

"Dammit Hunter, do I need to put a bell on you?"

"You can try. You know, if you had agreed to five a.m., you'd have plenty of time to shower."

"And get hardly any sleep?" I snorted. "No thanks. What do you want?"

His eyes flashed as he stalked closer, a rumbling sending shivers racing up my spine.

"You already know what I want, little mate."

I squealed and raced into the bathroom, tugging off my shirt and flinging it at him before hiding behind the door and trying to stifle a giggle.

"Now, now, little mate, don't you want help washing?"

Yes, my inner wolf panted.

Down, girl.

Mate! my wolf growled, sending a wave of heat rushing through me as Hunter's scent invaded my senses.

"I can smell your desire, Everly."

I whimpered, giving away my location, much to Hunter's delight as he rushed around the door and grinned at me, eyes dilating at the sight of me in just my underwear. He stalked forward, reaching around me to turn on the shower, his eyes never leaving my face.

"I thought you needed to shower," he whispered in my ear, sending another shiver of desire racing through me.

"Yes."

He quirked an eyebrow, his eyes skating down my nearly naked body.

I gulped before straightening my shoulders and grinning at him. Slowly, I tugged my sports bra off, tossing it to the side before turning and wiggling out of my panties, making sure to wiggle my ass a little more than was strictly necessary. He'd tortured me earlier, so it seemed only fair to even the balance. After all, as a Watcher, ensuring the balance was kept was my job.

Hunter growled and stepped closer, pressing himself against my back as I straightened up. The feel of his deliciously erect cock pressing against my ass had me moaning before I pulled away.

"I need to shower."

"Of course. So do I."

I grinned at him as I slipped into the shower, quirking a finger at him in invitation. He smirked and stripped down, standing before me in all his nude glory. *Damn. How did I get so lucky?*

I was snapped from my drooling observation by him stepping into the shower with me, crowding me until I was leaning against the back wall, the water beating down on his back. He dipped his head down, nuzzling my neck. The feel of him there, offering his strength, was almost too much to handle, reminding me of everything I had gained, and all I stood to lose if the council found me guilty for whatever imagined offense they came at me with.

A sob caught in my throat, followed by another. Before I knew it, a stream of tears were racing down my face.

Hunter snatched a sharp breath and then another calmer one before turning me to face him, his hands cradling my face.

"Everly, you can't let Giovanni's accusations get to you. You have to be strong, for yourself and for the rest of us. We'll figure out a way to prove your innocence and stop the Oberon, I promise."

I nodded, tears still streaming down my face.

"I know," I whispered. "It's just…it's all so overwhelming. The council, the Oberon, my mother… It's like I can't catch a break. And now I might lose everything, my wolf, my powers. I might even die."

Hunter wiped away my tears with his thumbs, a fierce look in his eyes.

"That will not happen, Everly. We will not let it happen. You are the strongest, bravest person I know, and you can handle anything that is thrown your way. And even if the worst does happen, we will face it together. You are not alone, little mate."

I sniffled and threw my arms around Hunter's neck, clinging to him for dear life.

"Thank you, Hunter. I don't know what I would do without you. Without all of you."

He chuckled and hugged me back.

"You'll never have to find out, little mate. I'll always be here for you, no matter what."

We stood there for a while, holding each other and drawing strength from each other's presence. Eventually, I pulled back and wiped my eyes, determined to put on a brave face.

"Okay, I'm ready. Let's go talk to Blade and figure out a plan."

Hunter grinned and kissed my forehead. "That's my girl. Let's do this. But first..." A twinkle in his eye, he held up my loofa.

I chuckled at the sight, obeying as he gestured with one hand for me to turn around.

Hunter helped me to soap up and started to wash me, his strong hands massaging my scalp and working their way down my back. I closed my eyes and let out a sigh of pleasure, the tension from the past days melting away under his touch. He continued to wash and massage me until I was fully relaxed, his hands moving over every inch of my body until I was practically purring with contentment.

"Is that better?" he asked, his voice low and husky.

"Mmm, much better," I replied, leaning into him and nuzzling his neck. "Thank you, Hunter."

He chuckled and kissed the top of my head, holding me close as the water cascaded over us. I couldn't help but feel grateful to have him in my life, to have all of my mates in my life. They may drive me crazy at times, but I knew that they would always be there for me, no matter what. And right now, I needed their support more than ever, with the council summons hanging over my head.

But for now, I was content to enjoy this moment with Hunter, to let go of my worries and just be in the present. And as long as he was by my side, I knew that I could face anything that came my way.

I sighed and pulled back, stepping out of the shower and drying off, ready to face the day.

Hunter dropped a kiss on my head before heading off to deal with his own duties. Wolf Lake Reno and Repair didn't work unless he did, after all.

I made it to the bookshop a little after ten, but thankfully Camille was there already opening.

"Sorry I'm late," I said, as I hurried through the doors.

"You don't have to apologize to me, you're the boss, remember?" Camille said with a smile from behind the counter.

"Right. Still getting used to that."

She hummed in response before turning back to stocking the shelves. I took my place behind the counter, opening the planner kept there to see what needed my attention today. Thankfully, it wasn't much.

"Hey, Cam?"

"Yes?"

"Blade is picking me up at lunch. We have to go over some stuff for an upcoming council meeting."

"Oh? Which council?"

"Balance Council."

She paused mid-way to slotting a book onto the shelf and glanced over her shoulder at me.

"It's odd for them to want to meet so soon into your career."

I grimaced and shrugged, not wanting to drag Camille into the drama of my summons. She shrugged back and resumed her work.

We fell into a companionable silence, both getting lost in the rhythm of the store.

I was deep in the stacks of the bookshop, organizing a new shipment of romance novels, when I heard the bell above the door jingle. I turned to see Blade leaning against the doorframe, his arms crossed and a frown on his face. I'd been expecting him, of course, but the look on his face sent a skitter of apprehension racing down my spine.

"Hey, what's wrong?" I asked, moving towards him.

"We need to talk," he said, his voice grim.

I nodded and followed him out of the shop, leaving the store in Camille's care. He led me to his car, and we drove in silence to the library. We made our way to the secret room, which was accessed by a kind of magic portal. Blade once described it as a pocket dimension, but the ins and outs still confused me. As always, the breadth of the space left me speechless. It was larger than the actual library that housed it.

Once we were seated at one of the study tables, Blade turned to me and sighed.

"Everly, as you know, you've been summoned to face the council," he said, his voice heavy.

"What I don't get is why. You said last night that it had to do with the increased Oberon attacks, but how does that involve me?" I asked, a tremor in my voice despite my attempts to quash it.

"It's not what you've done, it's what they're accusing you of not doing," Blade said, running one hand over my arm. "The Oberon have been attacking more frequently, and Giovanni, another Watcher on the council, is blaming you for the loss of life."

"That's ridiculous! I had nothing to do with those attacks," I exclaimed, anger surging through me. I couldn't believe what I was hearing. How could they possibly blame me for something I had no control over? I didn't even know about the supernatural world until I came to Wolf Lake.

"I know that, and you know that, but we have to be careful about how we handle this," Blade said, his voice calm and measured. "If they find you guilty, the consequences could be severe. Like I said, they could bind your wolf and your powers, which would ultimately kill you, given the strength of your wolf."

Tears sprang to my eyes at the thought of losing my life over something that I didn't even know existed until coming here. It was just… Dammit, it was *unfair*. And I'd be damned if I was going to take it lying down.

"I won't let that happen," I said, determination fueling my words.

"*We* won't let it happen," Blade said, his voice fierce. "But we have to be careful. Giovanni has it out for you, and I have a feeling there's more to this than meets the eye. I just can't put my finger on it yet."

I nodded, understanding what he meant. We couldn't go against the council lightly, but we also couldn't let them railroad me without a fight.

"We'll figure this out," I said, determination filling me. "We have to."

CHAPTER THREE

I barely remembered my head hitting the pillow after all the things Blade crammed into my mind that afternoon, so when strange, distorted visions and memories from the past overtook my mind, trepidation raced through me.

Scenes flashed before me, inundating me with information that I couldn't even begin to absorb. I tried to grab onto the different scenes whenever I saw something familiar, but everything was beyond my control. The scenes flashed and spun and twirled until I was nauseous. After what felt like forever, the lights and sounds settled into something resembling reality.

I was running through a field, chasing after a figure in the distance. As I got closer, my heart stuttered in recognition. It was my grandmother. She looked young and vibrant, like she had when we first started talking so long ago, not the weak and fragile woman I had seen on the video call before she passed.

"Everly, help me!" she called out, her voice carrying on the wind.

I tried to pick up my pace, but my legs were heavy and sluggish, like I was running through quicksand.

"Grandma, what's wrong?" I called out, panting from the effort of fighting whatever force was holding me back.

She turned to me, her face contorted in fear.

"They're coming for me, Everly. They want to take me away. You have to find me first."

"Who is coming?" I shouted, my heart racing with fear. "Take you where? Where are you? How do I find you?"

"You need to hurry! Help me. Save us, Everly. You're our last hope."

"Save you from what? Grandma, talk to me."

Before she could answer, the ground beneath us started to shake. I stumbled and fell to my knees as shadows started to swallow up my grandmother, eating away at her features until there was just a gaping maw of shadow.

"No!" I screamed, reaching out for her.

But it was too late. The shadows consumed her, and then, in a flash, she was gone.

I woke with a start, my heart pounding in my chest. It took me a moment to realize it was just a dream, but the fear and desperation lingered long after I opened my eyes. Just another nightmare. With a sigh, I laid my head back down, intent on returning to sleep while I had the chance.

This time, my dreams were just as strange, but no longer were the characters in them familiar. At least, not at first.

Shadowy figures were flooding from the trees surrounding a rugged camp. There were people and wolves fighting, snarling and slashing at the shadowy creatures. A woman was throwing balls of light at the shadows, and when the light touched them, they collapsed, the shadows melting away to reveal people underneath. I watched in horror as the gaunt faces of people trapped in the shadow were revealed. The wolves and people herded the shadows closer towards the woman, trapping them while she targeted them with her light.

Once the shadows were peeled from their hosts, some of the people dragged the gaunt figures off to the side. Things were so efficient that I found hope blooming in my chest. *Maybe we can do something like this to battle the Oberon.*

Ghost Wolf appeared beside me. I looked over at her, trying to make sense of everything as the scene played out before me.

"What's going on?" I asked, my voice shaking with equal parts hope and fear.

"This is a memory from my first human, so long ago," she replied, her voice soft. "It's important that you understand what happened."

"What does it mean?" I asked, my fear and confusion growing.

"I believe those overtaken by the Oberon can be saved, if you act quickly enough," she said, her eyes intense. "We need to question those who were rescued from the shadows during the previous battle to learn more."

The scene changed, showing a large, hulking man. He was physically handsome, but his twisted features hinted at a cruel depth that made me shiver.

"What's this?"

"Watch," Ghost Wolf said, nodding towards the man.

It was another memory, or something similar. The handsome man was large and imposing. I got the feeling that he wasn't human, but the men he was speaking with were. They were talking about needing wolf pelts. The man grew angry and yelled at the humans, unease skittering up my spine at the somewhat familiar sound of his voice.

"You useless fools!" the man bellowed. "If you can't catch the last shadow moon daughter, then what good are you to me?"

One of the humans, a brave or foolish man, spoke up. "But sir, we've tried everything. The moon daughter is elusive and always one step ahead of us."

The large man's face contorted in rage and he snapped the neck of the man who had spoken out. The other humans cowered in fear.

"You will bring me the moon daughter, or suffer the same fate," the man spat out.

The humans promised results and retreated hastily.

Once they had left, a twig snapped, drawing the large man's attention. It was a younger Ghost Wolf, who growled threateningly at him. He chuckled, the sound sending shivers racing through me at the familiar tone. A niggling in the back of my mind told me that I had met this being before, but no recollections have surfaced, so I focused instead on the scene playing out before me.

"Don't worry, little wolf," he said, his voice dripping with malice. "I'll have all the delicious magic in your pelt soon enough. Then none will be able to stand before me, or guard that which hides in your domain."

Shadows flicked around the man and he disappeared, leaving me terrified.

"What was that, Ghost?"

She growled, ruffling her coat as something flashed behind her eyes.

"Ghost?"

"There is more to learn this night. Watch."

The scene changed again, and I found myself outside of Wolf Lake Manor, the old folks home where my grandmother passed away. Shadows were streaming from the trees, attacking the residents. One of them, I realized with a jolt, was my grandma.

She stood before them, her shoulders squared, like a woman prepared to battle for her life. A shadow lunged for one of the residents behind her, and she snarled, the sound making my heart thump. *This is who Grandma really was. A warrior.*

It seemed like she was winning, as she exchanged blow after blow with the shadows, but then more came racing from the trees, surrounding her. She snarled, and a spark of light flashed from her palm before flittering out. The shadows circled closer, herding her towards the trees. She glanced back desperately before trying to summon another ball of light. This one, too, flashed before sputtering out of existence.

The grating sound of that shadowy monster who seems to control the others made me jump.

"Such a valiant attempt, Watcher. Don't worry, I'll make sure you suffer."

"Back, Oberon! Go back to where you came from!" she shouted, finally conjuring a small ball of flickering light and tossing it at the larger shadow.

The shadow cackled and lunged for her when the light bounced off its writhing darkness, its clawed hand closing around Grandma's arm. She snarled at him, thrashing and trying to pull away, but he bent closer to her and inhaled, and she went limp in his shadowy arms.

I screamed in horror, waking up with a start, my heart racing as I sat up in bed, panting and covered in sweat. I couldn't shake the feeling of dread that settled in my stomach, the memory of the shadows dragging my grandmother away still fresh in my mind.

Blade, Hunter, and Glenn rushed into the room, each searching for the threat. When they found none, Glenn gathered me into his arms, trying to soothe me as I sobbed uncontrollably.

"It was just a dream," he whispered, stroking my hair. "Just a dream, Silver."

But I knew it was more than that. The dream had felt so real, and the memory of the shadows attacking the old folks home, taking my grandma away, was still too fresh in my mind.

"Ghost Wolf was there," I managed to get out between sobs. "She said... she said that those overtaken by the Oberon can be saved, if we act quickly enough. We have to talk to those who were rescued from the shadows during the previous battle. We have to find out more."

My mates exchanged a worried look, clearly realizing the gravity of the situation.

"We'll do whatever it takes to help," Blade said, his voice resolute. "We'll figure this out, Everly."

I nodded, feeling a little bit of hope start to rise within me. With my mates by my side, I knew we could face anything.

I snuggled down into Glenn's arms, praying for a dreamless sleep.

*

Over breakfast the next morning, I was forced to confront the terrible images from my dreams.

Glenn was flipping pancakes on the griddle, a task he took on with enthusiasm, as we discussed what I'd seen.

"I saw a large man meeting with a group of humans," I said, stirring my coffee. "They were talking about needing wolf pelts. The man got angry and yelled at the humans, telling them that if they didn't hunt down the last moon daughter, then he no longer had use for them."

"That's not good," Blade said, his brow furrowing in concern. "Were the dreams prophetic?"

"No, more like memories from Ghost Wolf and her human half in her last life. But then he snapped the neck of one of the humans who talked back," I added, shuddering at the memory. "The other humans promised results and ran off."

"We need to find out who this man is and what he wanted with the moon daughter," Hunter said, his voice low and brooding.

"Yeah, and we need to figure out how this ties in with current events," Glenn said, flipping a pancake expertly. "No doubt that Ghost Wolf wouldn't have showed you this if it didn't have something to do with what's going on now."

"Agreed," Blade said. "We need to gather more information and try to decipher Everly's dreams. They could be crucial to surviving the Oberon."

I nodded, grateful for my mates' support. We spent the rest of breakfast discussing our game plan and trying to come up with a strategy.

I enjoyed the casual touches from each of my mates as we tried to move the conversation on to something a little less morbid. Blade was still frowning, but at least he wasn't bombarding me with questions I didn't have the answers to.

"Earth to Blade," I said, smirking when he shook his head.

"Sorry, just thinking. You mentioned that the voice of the shadow man was familiar, right?"

I shuddered at the memory. "Yeah, but I don't know why. I've been trying to place it, but it's like there's this disconnect in my mind."

Hunter frowned, sharing a look with Blade. Neither man spoke, instead shoving bites of food in their mouths.

"Don't worry, Silver," Glenn said, stroking my hand. "We'll figure this all out. We're a team."

I nodded, glad that they truly were acting like a team for once. At least when it counted, I could trust my mates to work together. It was definitely an improvement from Hunter's decision last month to go off half-assed on his own and try to play hero. I shuddered at the memory of almost losing my brooding mate to the disease that is the Oberon. I still had nightmares about that day. Then again, what *wasn't* I having nightmares about?

After we finished breakfast, Blade and Hunter huddled in the corner, whispering to each other. I couldn't help but feel a twinge of suspicion, but I was too tired to bother interrogating them. They probably just had some wolf business to discuss.

Glenn and I cleaned up the kitchen together, chatting about our plans for the day. He was going to meet with some pack members to discuss security measures, and I was supposed to head into my shop.

As we finished up, each of my mates gave me a kiss on the cheek, head, or hand before heading out for the day. It was a small gesture, but it made me feel loved and protected, quite the difference from the denial I was sporting not too long ago.

But as I thought about my dream and the large man's threats, I knew I couldn't go to work today. I needed to focus on finding out more about what was going on. I called Camille and asked if she could work without me for the day. She readily agreed, reminding me that I was the boss, after all—which I was pretty sure I would never get used to.

I decided to look into grandma's files for a clue about what was going on. She had always been a wealth of knowledge, and I hoped that she had left something behind that could help me understand my dreams better.

I sat at her desk, surrounded by piles of papers and old documents that I pulled out from the storage closet where the cleaning service had shoved them. I had no idea where to start, so I just began flipping through the pages randomly.

As I read through her notes and records, I began to piece together a story. Grandma had been working to uncover the origins of the Oberon and how the shadowy creatures came to be. She suspected that they were infected people who were overtaken by some shadowy disease. In her notes, she mentioned that she thought her light could save them. From the looks of things, she was working tirelessly to find a cure for the disease, though the notes cut off abruptly about a month before when she was said to have been taken to Wolf Lake Manor.

I was in awe of her strength and dedication, and I felt a renewed sense of purpose. I knew that I had to carry on her legacy and do everything in my power to discover the truth about the Oberon and figure out how to save the people infected by it. I can't help but wonder just who could be saved, and if it was truly possible. Was Grandma still out there somewhere, trapped by shadows and monsters, waiting for me to decipher her ramblings and everything else so I can bring her home? I didn't dare hope.

I spent the rest of the day lost in my grandmother's files, reading every piece of information I could find. And as I did, I began to understand my dreams better and see a path forward. I was determined to protect the ones I loved and defeat the darkness that threatened us all.

Whatever it took.

WOLF'S DUTY

CHAPTER FOUR

Hunter, Blade, and Glenn came home to find me lost in my grandma's files, which were now scattered all over the living room floor. They coaxed me out for dinner, and I reluctantly agreed. Starving myself didn't help anything, and I had a feeling I was going to need my strength to face whatever was coming.

As we sat on the couch, Blade shot me a smoldering look and crouched at my feet, then took one between his hands and started to run his thumbs over the sole. A moan slipped from my lips as he deepened the massage, and heat began to pool between my legs. I was helpless to resist the primal attraction to my most stoic mate when he was touching me like this, but I tried to focus on the conversation.

"So, how was your day?" I asked Blade, which was a valid question, if a little clichéd. His work in fire rescue could be physically demanding and emotionally taxing, as if he didn't have enough to worry about with his pack to run, and now, apparently, my life to save. Also, it was hard to think of anything more substantial while he was turning me into a puddle of relaxation. A puddle of *horny* relaxation.

"It was okay," he replied, his strong hands expertly rubbing my feet. "But I spent a lot of it researching the history of the Oberon."

"Really? What did you find out?" I asked, my voice hoarse, but if he noticed—and I was quite sure he did—he didn't acknowledge the need coursing through me.

"Well, the Oberon has been around for centuries," Blade said. "It's a powerful force of darkness that preys on the weaknesses of humans and wolves. It's been causing destruction and chaos for as long as anyone can remember."

"That's so scary," I said, shivering at the thought.

"Yeah, but we can't let it win," Blade said, determination in his voice. "We will do whatever it takes to defeat it and protect the packs."

I nodded, feeling the same sense of purpose. As we continued to chat, Glenn and Hunter prepared dinner together in the kitchen. I couldn't help but watch them with a sense of longing, knowing that I was equally attracted to both of them.

It was hard to fight my attraction to my mates, but I knew that we had bigger things to worry about. Still, I couldn't help but wonder what it would be like to give in to temptation and explore my desires with all three of them. One thing was for sure, we were a team, and we would do whatever it took to protect the packs and defeat the Oberon.

Glenn called out to us that dinner was ready, and Blade and I followed him out to the porch where a small table was set up from before I even came here. We sat down to enjoy the warm summer evening and the delicious meal that Glenn and Hunter had prepared.

As we ate, Blade went into more depth about his suspicions regarding the Oberon.

"I found some references to the Oberon in some old books I read," he said, pausing to take a bite of his food. "The first reference was around the time of the first pack forming, but it wasn't called the Oberon back then. It was just referred to as 'The Darkness.' There are hints in the books that Oberon is a person, not a disease, but I can't confirm it."

"A person?" I said, feeling a sense of worry wash over me. "Do you think it's someone we know?"

"I don't know," Blade said, shaking his head. "It's hard to say. The information is really vague and scattered. But I think it's worth investigating further."

Hunter and Glenn nodded in agreement, asking questions here and there to clarify things. As we discussed the situation, I couldn't help but feel a sense of unease. The thought of a powerful person working against us was scary, and I didn't know if we would be able to defeat them. The image of that cruel man flashed before my eyes, but I didn't want to jump to conclusions, so I just focused on my food.

Once we all finished eating and cleared the plates, we settled into what space wasn't covered in papers in the living room.

"I have some news," Hunter said, his voice grave, cutting across one of Blade's musings about the Oberon, and our non-existent plan to defeat it.

"What is it?" I asked, feeling a sense of dread wash over me.

"My father, you haven't met him, but he's the former alpha of the Shadow Keeper pack, has been working with the people who you released from the shadows of the Oberon when you were attacked last month," Hunter said.

"Working with them?" I asked, trying to wrap my head around the situation. "How?"

"He was trying to help them recover and regain their memories," Hunter said, his voice heavy with emotion.

"And?" I prompted, feeling a sense of impatience.

"Most of them don't seem to remember anything. They just remember living their lives as normal, and then a gaping hunger overtook them."

"A hunger for what?" Glenn asked, his brow furrowed in concern.

"They don't know," Hunter said. "But when the hunger got strong, their minds would go blank."

"What does it mean?" I asked, wrapping my arms around myself as a sudden chill settled over me.

"I don't know," Hunter said, shaking his head.

"Maybe," Blade said, stroking his chin thoughtfully, "it means they would just do whatever the Oberon wanted them to do, without questioning it. You said that the first Oberon to attack you seemed to hesitate, right, Everly?"

"Yeah. I almost got the sense that they didn't want to hurt me, like something was holding them back."

"Perhaps there's a point at which they lose themselves, and that one wasn't far enough gone yet to obey blindly."

"But how do we determine if that is correct if none of them remember what happened when they were under the influence of the shadows?" I asked, worrying at my lip. Glenn reached up and teased it loose from my teeth, smoothing his thumb over it.

"One of the people said they remember more," Hunter continued. "But they're afraid to speak of it. They said that 'he' would come for them if they talked about it."

"Who is 'he'?" Blade asked, his voice low and menacing.

"I don't know," Hunter said, shaking his head. "But I have a feeling that it's someone we need to be very wary of."

"We have to find out. We need to question these people further and see if we can get them to remember more. It could be the key to defeating the Oberon," Blade stated, pacing between my stacks of boxes.

We sat in silence, trying to process this new information. It was clear that we had a lot more work to do in order to defeat the Oberon. We were going to get to the bottom of this, no matter what it took. We couldn't let the Oberon win.

I glanced at Glenn to find him frowning up at the ceiling, seemingly deep in thought.

"What's wrong, Glenn?"

He turned to smile at me, but his eyes were far away.

"Everly?"

"Yes, Glenn?"

"Tell me about your dream again. The one with the man."

"Uh, okay, let's see. He was a tall, imposing man. But handsome in the way that humans usually aren't, y'know?"

Glenn nodded, encouraging me to continue while Hunter and Blade watched us with matching frowns. I'd have thought their jealousy was cute, if the notion that I could be attracted to anyone other than the three of them wasn't utterly ridiculous.

I cleared my throat. "Right. Well, uh, he was yelling at the group of humans. I think they were trappers. Ghost Wolf was there, at the end, so it must've been around that time, when the packs first formed, since she's been gone since then until she merged with me."

"Right, that makes sense. What else?"

"He was rambling about needing the last moon daughter," I noticed that all three men shared a look at this, like the words held some meaning that I hadn't yet picked up on. "One of the men tried to stand up to him, sort of, and he snapped his neck like it was nothing. The strength he must've had to do that." I shivered at the memory, then swallowed and made myself continue.

"His voice was almost familiar, like I'd heard it, or something like it, before. When the humans left, Ghost Wolf broke a twig. I'm not sure if it was intentional or not, and she's not very forthcoming with details. But the man didn't try to chase her or anything, he just told her 'Don't worry, little wolf, I'll have all the delicious magic in your pelt soon enough. Then none will be able to stand before me, or guard that which hides in your domain.' And that was it."

I frowned, watching as Glenn processed the information.

"Nothing else?"

"Well, he disappeared."

"How?"

"I mean, he sort of, faded? Or I guess the shadows like ate him and then he just sort of, wasn't there anymore. Does that make sense?"

Glenn's eyes flashed as he smiled.

"I'll be right back."

I glanced at Hunter and Blade, both of whom were watching the stairs where Glenn disappeared, a curious look on Hunter's face and a frown on Blade's.

Glenn raced down the stairs, a canvas in his hands. He placed it on the mantle and stepped back, and I gasp as it came into view.

"That's him," I said, voice shaking. It was the man from my dream, with the shadows writhing about his person.

"I dreamed of him, too," he said, his face dipping into a frown. "I had to paint it. I had the dream last night too, not long before your scream woke us up. I finished the painting during the day, but I didn't realize until now that it might be the same man. I had this feeling that I was forgetting something important, that's why I wanted you to go over your dreams again."

We stood there in silence, staring at the painting in shock. It was clear that everything was all connected to this man in some way, but we didn't know why or how.

"What do you think it means?" I asked, my voice barely more than a whisper.

"I don't know," Glenn said, shaking his head. "But I have a feeling that it's important. We need to figure out who he is and what he wants."

"And what about the shadows?" Blade asked. "What do they mean?"

"I don't know," I said, feeling a sense of dread wash over me. "But it feels so familiar. Like I should know exactly who and what I'm looking at."

We lapsed into silence once more, the grim visage of the man who was sure to haunt my nightmares in the coming days staring back at us. *What are we going to do about this mess?*

Glenn glanced at me, a frown once again marring his beautiful face.

"You should get some rest, Everly."

"I know. I just," I waved my hands around, indicating everything, "there's so much. With the council meeting looming before us, I feel like I need to do more. Learn more. Blade told me about their more specific reasonings for the summons, and part of me feels like they're right. Like it's my fault that so many people have been lost to this threat."

He moved to refute my words, but when I held my hand up, he snapped his mouth shut.

"I know that it's not *really* my fault, but it feels like it is. Like I should have already figured everything out by now. I'm supposed to be The Watcher, protecting our region from everything big and bad and mediating disputes between the packs, but instead I'm just...what? Playing at bookkeeper? Playing at mate. I've accomplished nothing since coming here besides convincing myself that I'm not crazy...and honestly, the jury's still out on that one for a whole other reason right now."

Hunter growled and crouched before me, Blade sliding onto the couch and lifting my feet onto his lap to resume his massage from earlier.

Hunter touched his fingertips to my face, gently turning me so he could stare into my eyes.

"You are not at fault. You are not *playing* at anything. You're learning and growing. People who grow up here are trained from birth to take up their responsibilities within the pack, but you have had everything thrust upon you and have been pressured to learn a lifetime of knowledge and skills in a mere fraction of the time that others are given."

I deflated as his words rattled around in my skull. He was right, of course, he usually was, even when I didn't want to admit it. That didn't change the guilt, though.

"He's right, Everly. You need to give yourself some slack. We're helping you. You don't need to take everything on yourself."

"I know, Blade. I know. I just feel so tired. And lost. I know I need to take up my duties as Watcher, and I'm starting to understand just what those duties are, thanks to you three, but it's still overwhelming."

"We'll be here for you, Everly. Let's just take things one day at a time. We still have a few months until the summit. You'll be ready, we'll make sure of it." Glenn's words offered a little more reassurance, but his hands falling on my shoulders and massaging the tension that had built up there over the day was what really had me relaxing and agreeing with their sentiments.

Maybe I was being too hard on myself. Still, I had duties and I needed to learn how to deal with them.

Patience, Everly. We will take our place in time. For now, you must focus on learning to harness the powers granted to you from your position, your heritage, and my gifts.

Of course, Ghost Wolf. Thank you.

Rest. We're safe with our mates.

I decided to take her advice, letting my men take care of me as I drifted off into a thankfully dreamless sleep.

CHAPTER FIVE

I woke up at six a.m., feeling barely rested and definitely not ready for the day ahead. But the day was coming for me, whether I was ready for it or not. With a groan, I got changed and headed downstairs to grab some breakfast before my seven a.m. training with Hunter.

When I got to the kitchen, I was surprised to find that Hunter wasn't there. Instead, Blade was sitting at the table, munching on a bagel.

"Good morning," he said, smiling at me. "I made you a bagel with cream cheese and some tea. I figured you might need a little pick-me-up before your training."

"Thanks, Blade," I said, gratefully accepting the food and drink. "I really appreciate it."

"No problem," he said, standing up and stretching. "I have some pack business to deal with, so I have to head out. But I'll see you later, okay?"

"Okay," I said, giving him a hug. "Take care of yourself."

I couldn't help but admire Blade's ass as he strode out of the door, then turned my attention back to my bagel. I was starving, and I knew that I needed to fuel up for my training. Hunter might have been a good teacher, but he wasn't a forgiving one, always running me through my paces.

As I finished my breakfast, I headed outside to find Hunter waiting for me. He gave me a quick inspection, frowning at whatever he saw.

"Is something wrong?" I asked, worried that I had somehow failed to meet his expectations.

"No, it's nothing," he said. "I just want to make sure you're ready for our training. It's going to be intense today."

"I'm ready," I said, determination in my voice. "Bring it on."

After warming up, Hunter ran me through some drills, but my body and mind were sluggish, struggling to keep up with our normal pace. Hunter shook his head and stopped me before I fell into the next stance.

"This isn't working," he said with a sigh.

I was ready to protest when he held up his hand and motioned me forward. He wrapped his arms around my shoulders and pulled me closer, his pine and snow scent wrapping around me. I relaxed into his embrace, inhaling his scent.

"Maybe we should take a break today. Let's go for a walk."

"That sounds good," I said, nuzzling him.

He chuckled and wrapped my hand in his, leading me towards the trees as the sun tipped over their edges.

Hunter led me into the forest, his strong hand guiding me through the trees. I followed him, marveling at the beauty of the place. Even with it being in my backyard, the pure wonder of the forest still caught me by surprise. The sunlight filtered through the leaves, casting dappled patterns on the ground. The air was crisp and clean, filled with the scents of pine and earth.

As we walked, I couldn't help but feel grateful for the reprieve from training. It was nice to just take in the beauty of the forest and enjoy the moment, to lose myself in something as simple as fallen leaves and dappled trees.

"This is it," Hunter said, stopping in front of a clearing. "This is my favorite place in the forest. I come here when I need to clear my head."

As always, I had lost track of where we were the moment we stepped foot into the forest. That was something that I really needed to work on.

If you weren't always boxing me into a corner of your mind, we would be more connected, and you would never be lost.

I filed Ghost Wolf's information away for the future before pushing her back down. She went grudgingly, snorting at me as I brought my mind back to the moment at hand.

Hunter was standing in the clearing, grinning at me. He looked more relaxed than I had seen him in a long while.

I stepped into the clearing, my breath catching in my throat. It was a place of unbridled beauty, with tall trees rising up around us and a small stream trickling through the center. The grass was soft and green, a stark contrast to the rough bark of the trees.

I turned to Hunter, a smile on my face. "This is amazing," I said. "I can see why it's your favorite place."

"I'm glad you like it," he said, his eyes twinkling. "I thought you might enjoy a break from training. We can sit and relax for a while before we get back to it."

I nodded, grateful for the chance to rest. We sat down by the stream, watching as the water flowed past us. It was peaceful and serene, and I felt my worries melting away.

I was glad that Hunter had brought me here. It was a welcome respite from the intensity of our training, and I knew that it would help me refocus and be ready for whatever came next. Because this break couldn't last forever…but for now would be enough.

I was relaxing by the stream, enjoying the peacefulness of the forest when the feel of being watched overwhelmed me. I turned to see Hunter staring at me, an intense look on his face.

I caught his gaze and smirked, deliberately flicking my tongue over my lips.

"You know, the view would be better with a little more skin," I teased, shifting and lifting the edge of my shirt.

He growled, the tension between us suddenly crackling through the air as he looked at me with a longing that sent shivers down my spine.

Hunter stalked closer, crowding me with his body. I could feel the heat radiating off him, and I knew that I wanted him.

I licked my lips again, watching as his parted in response. When he didn't make a move, I grabbed his face, pulling his lips against my own. Hunter was demanding, but not controlling. He wanted me as much as I wanted him, and it was a heady feeling.

Mate.

I wrapped my arms around his neck, pulling him closer as the kiss deepened. It was like everything else melted away, and all that mattered was the two of us. I was lost in the moment, lost in the heat of his touch.

Eventually, we broke apart, panting and gasping for air. I looked up at Hunter, my eyes heavy with desire.

"I think we should get back to training," I said, my voice low and husky.

"You're right," he said, a smile playing at the corners of his lips.

But Hunter didn't pull away. Instead, he resumed kissing me, his lips exploring mine with a hunger that left me weak in the knees. I wrapped my arms around him, pulling him closer as I kissed him back.

We were both lost in the moment, consumed by the heat between us. I could feel the tension coiling in my stomach, the desire racing through my veins. I wanted him more than anything, and I knew that he wanted me, too. I hadn't marked Hunter when we first sealed the bond, since I didn't understand the meaning behind doing so at the time, but now I was filled with the urge to sink my fangs into his shoulder and leave a permanent sign of our bond, one that matched the mark he'd left on me.

He growled at the look in my eyes, holding me tight to his chest while ravaging my mouth.

We tore at each other's clothes, pulling them off until we were both naked. I gasped as the cool air hit my skin, but it was quickly replaced by the heat of Hunter's touch.

We were lost in the pleasure of each other's bodies. It was wild and intense, and I could feel myself being carried away on a tide of desire as

Hunter kissed his way down my naked flesh. Every dip and curve, he lathered with attention, kissing and nibbling away until he reached that place between my legs where I needed him most.

"You're so wet for me, little mate," he growled.

I groaned, letting my knees fall apart as he buried his face at my core. His lips teased as he kissed my nub, forcing wanton moans from my lips as he brought his tongue and fingers to the game, tasting and stroking me as he explored me in a way he hadn't yet had the chance with everything going on.

He drove me to the edge, and when I begged for more, he gave it, but he wasn't content to let me linger in my release.

He crawled back up my body with a satisfied grin, licking his lips, which were still wet with my juices.

"You're delicious, little mate," he assured me as he pulled me closer.

I groaned into his kiss, tasting my own arousal on his lips.

"More," I demanded, much to his delight.

He picked me up and carried me towards a large boulder beside the stream. I moaned as he pressed my back against it before kissing his way down my neck.

"Hunter," I moaned as he began fondling my breasts, tweaking the nipples before kissing away the slight pain.

I clung to Hunter, my fingers digging into his back as I cried out in pleasure. He thrust into me, without ever taking his hands or mouth from my body. He worked me like he'd been doing it his whole life, his movements fierce and urgent. I could feel myself being pushed to the edge once more, and I knew that I was about to fall. I bit my lip, trying to hold in the pleasure until I could see his eyes glazing over. He lifted his head and brushed my hair aside, nipping at my neck, sending a jolt racing right to my core.

The added sensation was more than I could handle as my body

shuddered with pleasure. I cried out as the orgasm washed over me, my body trembling with the intensity of it. Hunter followed me over the edge, his own release coming in a guttural groan when I bit down on his shoulder, leaving a mark of my own.

When our breathing began to steady, he laid his head against my own, a small smile on his face.

"That was wonderful, Hunter. My only complaint is that there's a stick digging into my ass."

He released a startled chuckle and helped me to find the offending stick, tossing it away. We washed up in the stream before tugging our clothes back on, Hunter keeping contact with me the whole time.

I was lying in the clearing with Hunter, basking in the afterglow of our steamy encounter, when I heard a familiar voice.

"Well, well, well. What do we have here?"

I turned to see Glenn standing at the edge of the clearing, a grin on his face. He sniffed the air and winked at Hunter before making a show of looking around.

"You've hoarded the fair lady long enough, Shadow Keeper. Let a guy spend some time with his mate, will ya?"

Hunter rolled his eyes and growled playfully, tugging me down for a hot kiss that left me panting and wanting a second go at him. When he pulled back, the intense look on his face was made less intimidating by a playful smirk. I kissed his cheek one more time before standing up and taking Glenn's hand.

Hunter smacked my ass as Glenn pulled me into his arms for a hug, making me squeal.

I couldn't help but feel a twinge of suspicion at the ease with which he handed me over, but I was too busy admiring my other mate to bother pursuing it.

"Come on, love," Glenn said, taking my hand and leading me away.

"Let's leave this grump behind and go have some fun."

I laughed, racing after Glenn as he jogged off into the trees.

"What are we doing today?" I asked between breaths.

"You'll see, Silver. Last one to the Lodge is cooking dinner!"

"Oh, you are on, wolf boy!"

I drew Ghost Wolf closer to the surface, channeling her strength to put on a burst of speed.

I laughed as my mind merged a little more with Ghost Wolf's, our essences growing closer together. The forest was different through the eyes of a wolf, and despite not having shifted, I was looking around through her eyes as we raced towards the neutral meeting place referred to as the Lodge, a gift from Hunter to me. Really, it was a gift from all three of my mates, but Hunter did the breadth of the work, while Blade financed it, and Glenn decorated.

I broke through the trees seconds before Glenn, pumping my fist victoriously in the air.

"Oh, sweet Silver, how fast you've gotten," he said with a grin, sweeping me into his arms and spinning me around.

I couldn't help but laugh, the feel of Glenn's arms around me lifting some heavy load that I didn't realize was still weighing on my mind.

"Why are we here, Glenn?" I asked again as he put me down.

"We're here, sweet Silver, to prepare the Lodge!"

"For what?"

"Well, there will be meetings with the packs before the summit, so I wanted to bring you here to pick out some other decorations and things. This is *your* place, and it needs your touch added."

"That sounds fun."

He grinned and grabbed my hand, tugging me inside.

We spent the rest of the day going over the different things that would be needed for mediations, gatherings, and even parties at the lodge, Glenn explaining what each one would require and why it might be held.

He had me scrolling through different cutlery, cooking supplies, party decorations, lawn furniture and more, but what really took me by surprise, was when he pulled up a link to his gallery and had me scroll through his paintings, choosing several that he promised to bring over, free of charge.

"I know you're my mate, Glenn, but you can't just go giving me million-dollar paintings for free."

"And why not, Silver? They're my paintings, so I get to decide their worth. If I decide that they belong here, in the lodge, who's to stop me?"

I rolled my eyes at his insistence, but ultimately relented, agreeing that many of the walls were a bit bare. The only art currently displayed was a large version of the sketch grandma had in her journal, of me and my three mates in wolf form—though it was one I never tired of looking at.

By the time we finished ordering things for the Lodge and arguing about whether or not Glenn was allowed to give his paintings away to me, the sun had set.

"Ready to head home?" he asked, a small smile on his face.

"Yeah, I'm beat. Which is odd, since I didn't do anything today," I said with a frown.

Glenn chuckled and shook his head, taking my hand in his.

"Do you call racing through the forest, kitting out a neutral meeting place, and training 'nothing'?"

"I didn't exactly train."

"No? You didn't stretch? Or connect with your wolf? Or practice using your other senses?"

His words made me narrow my eyes as I realize just how thoroughly I'd been played—by them both.

"Smooth, mate, very smooth."

He bowed with a flourish before grasping my hand again and planting a hot kiss on my knuckles. I groaned and shook my head, wrapping his hand in mine and tugging him up.

"Let's get home, you manipulative man. I seem to recall that you're cooking."

CHAPTER SIX

As we walked through the forest, Glenn's grip on my hand was firm and reassuring. Rather than taking me home, he led me to a secluded spot, where he had an easel set up, and a picnic spread out on a blanket. He had even brought a book for me to read, and I couldn't help but feel touched by the thought he put into this.

"I thought you might like a day away from training, and I figured this would be the perfect spot to spend it. I've been coming here for years, it's a special place for me," Glenn said, his eyes shining with excitement.

The space was breathtakingly beautiful. The sun was shining, the birds were chirping, and there were even a few animals watching us curiously. We were in a meadow filled with flowers, and in the distance, I could see mountains. I could imagine the mountains in fall, with snow-capped peaks. The meadow was filled with wildflowers of every shade, so many that I had never even seen before. It was amazing. I had never felt so at peace, and I couldn't help but smile at Glenn's thoughtfulness.

"Come, let me feed you," he said, gesturing to the spread on the blanket. He had brought sandwiches, fruits, and even a bottle of wine.

I settled down on the blanket and let him serve me. The food was delicious, and I couldn't help but feel grateful for this moment of peace.

After we finished eating, Glenn surprised me even further as he began kneading my shoulders with expert fingers, gently pushing me forward until I was lying face down, which allowed him to work his way down my back and legs, and if he lingered a little longer than necessary on my glutes, I certainly wasn't complaining.

Glenn made his way back up and worked on my shoulders, his hands expertly kneading the knots and tension out of my muscles. I let out a moan, enjoying the feel of his strong fingers, feeling my body slowly start to relax. He worked his way back down my back, once again. His touch was gentle but firm, and I could feel myself start to drift off into a state of complete relaxation.

When he finished, I turned over and thanked him, feeling refreshed and rejuvenated. He smirked and planted a kiss on my cheek, then he handed me the book he had brought for me, and I settled in to read, feeling the warmth of the sun on my face. I couldn't remember the last time I had felt this at peace, and I knew that I had Glenn to thank for that.

As I read, I couldn't help but reflect on how different Glenn was from my other two mates. Glenn was the peacemaker, the one who brought balance to our group. At the same time, he wasn't afraid to poke the wolves, so to speak, often antagonizing the others rather than settling things. He had a way of making me feel safe and cared for. Where Hunter was sarcastic and helpful, Glenn was soft and caring. Blade was more take-charge, always wanting to be in control or in the center of things. It still amazed me how three totally different men could put aside their differences to work together for me, even while butting heads.

It wasn't long before I got lost in the pages of my regency romance, and while I could feel Glenn's eyes on me, I was too absorbed in my novel to look up when he got up and moved to the side. The novel was like a temporary escape from reality, transporting me to a different time and place. The characters' struggles and romances were a stark contrast to my own chaotic life, and I found myself getting lost in their story of a more straightforward courting and romance.

I flipped the page and sighed happily.

My life might be more complicated, but I couldn't help but feel grateful for the three men in it. Each of them brought something unique and special to the table, and I knew that I was lucky to have them by my side.

I closed the book, feeling the sun on my face and the breeze in my hair. I looked to where Glenn was sitting, but he wasn't where I had left him. I glanced around, finding him back in the shade of the trees, sitting before an easel with a look of concentration on his face. I smiled, enjoying the sight of him deep in thought, and returned to my novel. Since I had gotten some time to relax, I better do just that.

As I read, I lost track of time, and before I knew it, the sun was setting, making my eyes water as I finished the last few lines of my book in the dimming light.

The setting sun cast an ethereal glow across the meadow. The shadows of the mountains created fantastical shapes, and fireflies were taking flight, adding to the magical atmosphere. I closed the book and set it aside, feeling a sense of peace and contentment wash over me.

Glenn came and sat beside me, resting his arm across my shoulders as the sun slowly dipped below the horizon, casting hues of pink, orange, and purple across the sky. The colors were mesmerizing, and I couldn't help but feel awestruck by the beauty of it all.

Glenn pulled me closer, and I leaned my head on his shoulder, feeling a sense of warmth and safety radiating from him. We sat there in a comfortable silence, the colorful hues gradually giving way to the twinkling of stars as we gazed towards the horizon.

It was moments like these, when everything else seemed to fade away, that I felt truly grateful for Glenn and our mateship. He had been the one to bring me to this beautiful spot, to give me a break from training, and to make me feel relaxed and rejuvenated. He had been the one to take care of me when I needed it, and I knew that I could always count on him to be there for me.

As the last rays of the sun disappeared behind the mountains, Glenn turned to me and smiled, a gentle look in his eyes. I smiled back, feeling a sense of contentment settle over me. I knew that no matter what the future held, my mates would go to the ends of the earth to keep me safe and happy. While I didn't want them putting themselves at risk for me, the fact that I knew they would brought about a sense of belonging that I'd never felt before.

Once the light of the sun had given way to the waning crescent moon, Glenn helped me to stand, pulling me in for a hug. We embraced for a long moment before he pulled back and began to gather up the remains of the day.

He placed the leftover food, the blanket, and my book in one large canvas bag, and his easel and painting supplies went into another. He carefully covered the painting, placing the canvas in the second oversized shoulder bag with the rest of his painting supplies before turning to me and holding out his hand. I felt a little guilty about him carrying everything, but when I moved to take one of the bags, he just laughed and kissed my hand.

The walk through the trees was peaceful, and I found that I was getting better at channeling my wolf's senses, allowing me to see in the dark. As we walked, I couldn't help but think about the painting Glenn had been working on. I was curious to see it, but I didn't want to push him, so I kept quiet, just enjoying the peaceful evening.

But once we arrived home, curiosity got the best of me. I turned to him and asked, "Can I see the painting you were working on earlier?"

He smiled and replied, "Of course, I'll show it to you when I have it all set up. But it's not quite finished yet."

I chuckled and shook my head.

"I'll try not to peek this time."

He carefully set down his supplies and turned to me with a wide grin, "I'm sure your dizzy spells have been miraculously cured."

"For now, let's get you inside and settled, it's been a long day," he said, holding out his hand.

I nodded, feeling a sense of exhaustion wash over me. I hadn't done much of anything today, but I was still drained. I knew that the training and stress of the council's impending summit was taking its toll on me, so I tried not to be too hard on myself.

With the support of our mates, everything will be fine.

Once we entered the house, I noticed that Hunter and Blade were nowhere to be found. I started to feel a twinge of anxiety, wondering where they could be and if they were safe, but before I could dwell on it for too long, Glenn suggested we make dinner together. He was so cheerful and playful, it was hard not to get caught up in his good mood—even if it was just an excuse to shirk half his cooking duties.

We decided on pizza. I was somewhat surprised that Glenn knew how to make pizza from scratch, but he was at ease in the kitchen. He moved like a pro, perhaps the confidence came from his penchant for art.

"I'm surprised you can cook so well, Glenn. I mean, steak is one thing, but fresh pizza?"

He chuckled and tossed a handful of flour at me, making me screech.

"Cooking is an art like any other...now baking, that's a science," he said, a twinkle in his eye as he flicked more flour at me.

"Oh, it is on!" I shouted, grabbing the excess flour and flinging it at him before ducking behind the counter.

Glenn barked out a shout of laughter, chasing me through the house and out onto the porch to douse me with more of the powdery ingredients. By the time he caught up with me, we were both laughing hysterically, and instead of splattering me with more flour, he scooped me up into his arms and swung me around, carrying me back into the kitchen and planting me at one of the barstools he had acquired when he moved in.

"Just let the master work," he said haughtily, making me laugh again.

It was just as mesmerizing watching him cook as watching him paint.

The pizza was, of course, delicious. We ate nearly the whole eighteen inch monstrosity between just the two of us.

After we finished eating, Glenn suggested we sit outside on the porch to enjoy the night. It was nice. I sat on the porch swing, sipping my cup of tea and staring up at the moon, while Glenn pulled out his easel and painting supplies.

"I want to finish my masterpiece," he said with a grin.

I couldn't help but feel curious as I watched him work, the way his brushstrokes were precise yet fluid, and how he seemed to be in complete control of his art. It was mesmerizing to watch him create something that would no doubt be beautiful, and I couldn't wait to see the finished product.

After a few moments, Glenn stood back and exclaimed, "Ta-da!"

He turned the canvas around to reveal a portrait of me reading my book in the meadow. The sun played on my hair and the glint in my eyes made me look ethereal. I was in awe, it was like he had captured a moment of pure magic. I almost couldn't believe that the woman in the painting was me.

"It's beautiful," I said, unable to find the words to express how much the painting meant to me. "Thank you."

"I'm glad you like it," Glenn said, a pleased expression on his face. "You looked so peaceful and content in that moment, I wanted to capture it forever."

We sat there for a while longer, staring at the painting and enjoying the quiet of the night. I couldn't help but feel grateful for the day and for the man sitting beside me. Glenn had not only captured a moment in time, but he had also captured a feeling. A feeling of contentment, safety and belonging, and I knew that I would always treasure that painting as a reminder of that special day.

As the night came to a close, Glenn escorted me up to my room. Once we reached my room, he pulled me into his arms, pressing his lips to mine in a searing kiss. It was a kiss filled with passion and longing, and it left me breathless.

Glenn's hands were tangled in my hair, pulling me closer as he deepened the kiss. I could feel the heat building between us, and I couldn't help but let out a moan of pleasure. I clung to him, feeling like I never wanted the kiss to end.

When Glenn pulled back, resting his forehead against mine and smiling, I let out a groan. I was half tempted to ask him to join me in bed, but he was right about me being exhausted.

"Good night, Silver," he said softly.

I smiled back, feeling a sense of warmth and contentment spread through me.

"Good night, Glenn," I whispered back. I leaned in for one more quick kiss before we said our final good nights, and I went into my room, closing the door behind me.

I lay in bed, replaying the kiss over and over. I couldn't wait for the next time I would be in Glenn's arms. The thought of it filled me with a sense of excitement and anticipation, and I knew that with him by my side, I could face anything that life threw at me.

CHAPTER SEVEN

The next morning, when I awoke and realized that Hunter and Blade still hadn't returned home, I couldn't shake off the feeling of unease that had settled in my stomach. I went in search of Glenn, and found him in the kitchen making breakfast.

"Glenn, have Hunter and Blade come back yet?" I asked him, trying to keep the worry out of my voice.

Glenn's expression grew somber as he shook his head. "No, they haven't."

I couldn't help but feel a sense of dread as I asked, "Why didn't they come back?"

"They had some pack business to take care of," Glenn said, avoiding my gaze. I narrowed my eyes at him while he studiously ignored them. Oh yeah, he knew more than he was letting on for sure, and I wasn't letting him off the hook that easily. I had a bad feeling about this.

"What kind of pack business?"

"It's complicated," Glenn said, turning away to get some milk from the fridge and staying there much longer than he needed to.

"What are you hiding, Glenn?" I asked, working hard to keep my voice calm but firm as I plucked the milk from his hands and put it on the counter.

He hesitated a moment, then sighed and leaned back against the counter behind him.

"Blade and Hunter went out of town to try and get some council members on their side before the meeting on September 1st."

I couldn't believe what I was hearing. "They went out of town without telling me? How could they do that? How long have they been gone?"

"They left yesterday after I stole you away from Hunter," Glenn said, still avoiding my gaze.

They'd planned it. They'd worked together to trick me. I swallowed the acrid sting of betrayal.

"Why didn't they tell me? Why didn't you?"

"They didn't want to worry you. They thought it would be better if you didn't know," Glenn admitted.

"Better for who?" I demanded, my voice raised in frustration. "This is my life, too. I have a right to know what's going on. They can't just make decisions like this without including me."

Glenn didn't have a response, and I could tell that he felt guilty for keeping this from me. I couldn't believe that my mates would keep something like this from me, especially with the council meeting coming up. I knew that this meeting would decide the fate of my future, we all knew it. I couldn't believe that they would make such a big decision without consulting me. That they didn't trust me to handle it was even worse than the fact they'd gone behind my back. Sure, I agreed that we needed help, but we were supposed to work as a team. The last time one of my mates went off without being honest with me, Hunter was nearly turned by the Oberon. Oh, gods, I hoped they were okay.

Glenn sat me down and put his hand on mine, trying to soothe me. "Everly, I know you're upset, and I understand why. But please try to understand that Blade and Hunter did this for us, for our future together." He paused for a moment before continuing. "Blade has grown suspicious about several members of the council potentially working with the Oberon. He thinks that if we don't get some council members on our side, we'll be outnumbered and outvoted at the meeting. It's a big risk they took, but they did it to keep us safe."

I listened to him, trying to understand where they were coming from. I knew that the council meeting was important and that we needed allies, but it was hard for me to accept that my mates would make such a big decision without consulting me first. "I get that they're trying to protect us, but they should have included me in this decision."

Glenn looked at me with understanding in his eyes. "I know, and I'm sorry. They didn't mean to hurt you. They just wanted to protect you, and they thought this was the best way to do it. But I promise you, they'll be back soon and they'll explain everything to you. And I'll make sure they include you in all future decisions."

I took a deep breath, trying to calm myself. I knew that Glenn was right, my mates did want to protect me, and I couldn't stay angry at them forever. But I couldn't shake off the feeling of betrayal. And when they got back, we would be having a serious conversation about communication and trust in our relationship.

I tried to shake the feeling off and focus on the matter at hand.

"Why did Blade suspect certain council members? And who are these council members?"

Glenn hesitated for a moment, clearly uncomfortable with the subject. "Blade has had his suspicions for a while now. He's worried that some members of the council may be working with the Oberon. He's been keeping a close eye on them, trying to gather evidence. But it's all just speculation at this point."

I couldn't believe what I was hearing. He'd suspected this and kept it from me, and then gone rushing off to risk himself and Hunter by walking right into the dragon's den. Calm, Everly, I reminded myself. Focus.

"Who does he suspect?" I eventually managed.

"Giovanni is his prime suspect," Glenn said, handing me a steaming mug, which I accepted with barely a glance. "He's been acting strange lately, and he's been making moves that don't align with the council's goals. But Blade thinks the corruption may go deeper than just Giovanni.

He's worried that there may be more council members involved."

My blood boiled at the thought of members of the council working with the Oberon. They were supposed to protect us, not betray us. "Why didn't they tell me any of this? Why did they go behind my back and investigate without me? We're supposed to be working as a team."

"They were trying to protect you, Everly," Glenn said, placing a hand on my shoulder. "They didn't want to worry you and they wanted to gather more information before bringing it to you. They wanted to be sure before accusing anyone. They didn't want to bring this to you until they had concrete evidence."

"Why is Blade so suspicious of the council members?" I asked, my voice tight with anger and frustration. "Which council members does he suspect? Other than Giovanni, I mean."

Glenn let out a sigh and looked at me with a serious expression. "Like I said, Blade's prime suspect is Giovanni, but he's worried that the corruption goes deeper than that. We don't have any evidence proving that others are involved, at least not any he's shown me. He thinks the whole meeting is a setup and that the Oberon might be planning to ambush us, at worst. He's worried that they might manipulate the vote to bind your wolf, at best." He blew out a frustrated breath. "We really don't know enough about the Oberon."

"No, we don't," I agreed, my breath leaving me in a heavy sigh as I wrapped my hands around my mug and stared into it.

Hearing those words had sent a chill down my spine. The thought of the council being in league with the Oberon was terrifying, and the idea that they might try to bind my wolf was even worse. That was a death sentence, since Treoirn was so strong. Even the best case scenario would result in my death.

"I understand why they tried to keep this from me," I said, my voice level, "and I get that you all want to protect me, but you can't shut me out of this. You need me. And how am I supposed to help if I don't know who the enemy is?"

"We don't know for certain that anyone besides the Oberon are the enemy."

"We need to know more about the Oberon," I growled in frustration.

Glenn nodded in agreement, pulling me into his arms. I remained stiff at first, but eventually melted into his comforting embrace. We had enough enemies without fighting each other.

Everything was piling up around me, and I didn't have the first idea how to deal with it all.

"What are we going to do, Glenn?" I muttered against his chest.

"We're going to keep gathering our resources, learning, and teaching you what you need to know."

"Do you have plans today?" I asked, pulling back to look up at him.

He shrugged and looked around.

"I should probably clean our little flour mess from last night."

I laughed, looking around for the first time since coming downstairs. It was true, the kitchen was covered in a fine layer of white dust, and the memory left a smile on my face.

It took us about an hour to clean the entire mess, but by the time we finished, the kitchen was sparkling. When we were done, I sank down into one of the kitchen table chairs, rubbing a hand down my face as Glenn insisted I sit and eat the now-cold eggs that he had prepared, not wanting me to start my day on an empty stomach.

"So," he said as I ate. "I have a perfectly good painting of my stunning mate going to waste. Any thoughts on where we should hang it?"

I couldn't help but roll my eyes. Yes, the painting was beautiful, but I wasn't exactly eager to stare at myself all the time.

"Tell you what... If you promise to make one of each of us, you can hang it on the bare wall of the living room. I don't want to just look at myself all the time."

Glenn grinned and nodded.

"Deal, Silver. I'll make one of each of us, and one of all of us... maybe, when I have time, I'll even make one of each of us with you for our rooms," he mumbled thoughtfully.

I stood, stretching, and wandered back upstairs to shower and dress.

Once I had pulled on a pair of ripped jeans and a button up blouse, I paused to inspect myself in the mirror. The woman before me was almost a stranger, with long, lustrous hair, a smallish waist, long legs and flared out hips. Her lips were pinched into a look of concentration while bright eyes stared back at me, eyes that swirled with undertones of silver and gold, like the wolf's spirit inside her was just below the surface.

I generally didn't see myself the way Glenn saw me, the way he painted me, but the woman staring back at me was definitely the same one he painted. There was a dark, cynical undertone to my eyes in this mirror, though, that he didn't catch in the painting. Perhaps it's because I was relaxed yesterday, whereas now, I was having to go out and face reality. A reality in which people and monsters wanted me dead.

I'd changed a lot since coming to Wolf Lake. No longer was I the scared girl, afraid of my own desires. Now I was the strong wolf shifter, learning about my duties and nearly ready to shoulder some of the responsibility my grandmother had hoped I would one day take over. And I was ready to face those people and monsters.

I felt the change in the air as Glenn poked his head in the room, grinning at me.

"You look amazing, as always, Silver."

Unbidden, a smile parted my lips, lighting up the face in the mirror as I took in Glenn's form in the shimmering surface. I wasn't the only one who had changed. My mates were working together, helping me as well as each other. It was amazing how much things had changed in one month.

I twirled around to face Glenn.

"What's that grin for, mate?"

"Come see for yourself," he said, before turning on his heel and hurrying downstairs.

I followed him, chuckling at his excitement. Downstairs, I found him fiddling with the now-framed canvas from last night. He had taped out spaces on the wall with painter's tape, where I assumed the other paintings I had requested would go. The one of me in the meadow was on the end, a plaque that said simple 'Everly' below it.

I moved closer, seeing plaques under the other spaces. Beside 'Everly' was 'Glenn.' Next to 'Glenn' was 'The Mate Circle,' and beside that was 'Hunter,' followed by 'Blade.' I smiled, excited by the prospect of paintings of all of us decorating the room where we tended to sit together in the evenings.

"Thank you, Glenn. I appreciate that you took my request seriously."

He chuckled and grabbed my hand.

"Anything for you, Silver. Now, what are your plans for the day?"

"I'm going to the shop. Blade has been going over the various Watcher duties with me, so I think I'll announce that I'm available for limited duties while I learn more about my responsibilities."

He frowned but nodded.

"That makes sense."

"If it makes sense, why don't you look happy?"

"Did you already discuss this with Hunter and Blade?"

I rolled my eyes, annoyed by his question. Perhaps if Hunter and Blade were around, instead of off trying to play hero, I could have discussed it with them. Instead of saying that, however, I turned and walked back towards the kitchen to fill my water.

"I didn't realize I needed their permission to do my job, Glenn."

I could feel his heat behind me, and didn't miss the flinch in his movements. My words may have been harsh, but they were true. The Watcher position was mine by birth, my duty, whether I had wanted it or not. Now that I was more comfortable with my role here in Wolf Lake, in the heart of the Shadow Moon territory, I wanted to take up the mantle and make a difference. I couldn't just sit back while a vital role was left unfilled.

"You don't need our permission to do anything, Everly. I just mean… are you sure you're ready? It's a lot of responsibility."

I blew out a breath, turning to face him and leaning my back against the fridge.

"Honestly? I'm not sure, Glenn, but I'll never be ready if I keep hiding from it. I learn best by doing, not reading. Blade's books are fine and all, but I'm a hands-on type of girl."

He nodded thoughtfully before tugging me into his arms.

"Of course, Silver. I'm just worried about you. This is all so new. I wish we could just hide away in the forest and not have to worry about any of this," he murmured against my head.

I sighed and leaned against him, nodding in agreement.

"Wouldn't that be nice?" I pulled back and stared in his expressive eyes. "Unfortunately, that's not an option. And since Treoirn thinks we have a chance to save the people infected…to save Grandma… I have to take it. I have to figure this out, Glenn."

"I know, Silver. I know. I'll be right beside you, whatever path you take. Just be prepared for Blade and Hunter to have hissy fits."

I couldn't help but giggle at the mental image of my stoic and sarcastic mates throwing tantrums like toddlers. Wouldn't that be a sight?

I pulled myself from Glenn's arms, kissing his cheek before turning towards the door.

"I'm off, Glenn. Have a nice day."

"You too, Silver."

CHAPTER EIGHT

Tension filled my body the whole drive to the shop. I kept expecting the Oberon, or the council, or some other unnamed threat to jump out at any moment. Thankfully, nothing did, but I still held the steering wheel in a white-knuckled grip until I pulled up and parked out front of my shop: Wolf Lake Books and Tea.

I had always dreamed of owning a bookshop, so when I got the letter saying that I had inherited Grandma's, I was simultaneously overjoyed at having a dream come true and devastated at losing Grandma without ever really knowing her. Of course, I hadn't realized that the shop came with so much baggage. Having duties beyond just running a bookstore was never part of my dream, but I couldn't say I was too upset. It brought me my mates, after all. And Camille. Despite her being nearly two years younger than me, we'd become close friends.

I glanced at the clock before turning off the car, slightly surprised to see that it was only half past nine. When I made it to the door, I wasn't shocked to find it still locked. We opened at ten, but Camille usually got here a little early to set everything up for the day. It looked like I had beaten her in, for once.

I unlocked the door and went about arranging the bakery display and filling the few blank spots on our book displays, humming to myself. Camille arrived around quarter past the hour, the first time that I was aware she'd ever been late. She rushed through the doors in a flurry, looking frazzled.

"I'm sorry I'm late, Everly. I got held up with pack stuff."

"Not a problem, Camille. It's not like we're rushed off our feet. Besides, you're never late and you never leave early. Have you even taken so much as a sick day since I arrived in Wolf Lake?"

She paused, thinking with an adorable frown on her face.

"You know, I don't think I have. That doesn't excuse my lateness, though."

I waved my hand dismissively in the air, finishing with the display I was working on before heading to the front desk to grab our ledger.

"Don't worry about it, Cam. I'm gonna go over some of the stuff I'm behind on. Shout if you need me."

"Right."

It took me until around one p.m. to go over the ledge, cataloguing the orders and checking on the expense report. By the time I finished, I was stiff and ready to move around. I stretched my aching back a moment before slinking out towards the main shop.

I leaned against the door to my office when I saw Camille talking with a customer, straining my wolf's senses to hear their conversation.

"...sure when things will be back to normal, Miss Derin."

"It's just that we've got a lot of minor disputes. The alphas are just as bad as the kids about who is at fault, I was really hoping we could get some help."

"I understand your frustration, I do, but Everly is still settling in. She wasn't raised within a Ley Boundary, so she doesn't understand everything that's going on yet."

"I know, dear, I know. I'm just so worried. If we don't deal with this, I'm afraid that the boys are going to start a war between the packs."

Camille raised her eyebrows, clearly a little startled by Miss Derin's words. She glanced back to see me standing there, a benign smile plastered on my face.

"I'm sure she's working hard to learn what she needs, but I don't..."

I took that moment to step forward. I hadn't had a chance to tell Camille of my decision to start easing into the Watcher position, but clearly it was the right one.

"Hello," I cut off Camille's uncertain excuse, "I'm Everly Anderson, Eustice Cummings was my grandmother."

"Oh, hello, dear." Her eyes flickered to Camille, a small frown on her face.

"What can I help you with…it's Miss Derin, right?"

"Er, yes. Well, I was just… Camille said that you might not be ready."

"Do you require me as the owner of this store, or as The Watcher of this county?" I asked softly.

Her eyes widened, her mouth flapping open and closed in shock.

"As I was saying, Miss Derin, Everly is still settling in. She didn't have a chance to get briefed on her role before Eustice left us."

"Of course, dear, of course. I was just hoping—"

"I don't think Everly is ready to take on any duties."

"Actually," I said, smiling softly at Camille so she knew she wasn't in trouble. "Blade has been working with me to make sure I'm prepared. I'm going to be starting off slow, but I will be taking on some of my Watcher duties in a limited capacity while I continue to learn the ropes."

A spark of hope flared in Miss Derin's eyes.

"Now, what did you need help with, Miss Derin?"

She cleared her throat and shot me a watery smile. "My boys, they've gotten into a bit of a…contest, I guess, with the Shadow Keeper pack. We're from Moon Walker. They've been at it for weeks with these boys from the Shadow pack, and I'm afraid it's just getting worse. I was really hoping that they could settle it on their own, but it's not looking like that. I went to the elder alphas of the two packs, but they're almost as bad as the children."

I chuckled and shook my head.

"I did get that there was a bit of animosity," I murmured. "Can you tell me more about the dispute?"

She huffed and rolled her eyes, her frail hands shaking. I glanced at

Camille, who nodded her head towards a little reading nook in the back corner of the store. It was out of the way, I'd guess for just this purpose. I smiled gratefully at her and gently took Miss Derin's elbow, leading her to one of the chairs before settling myself across from her.

"Now, please tell me what you can about the dispute, and then we can summon the people in question to deal with things."

"There's this lake, one of the smaller ones. It's on the edge of the Moon Walker and Shadow Keeper land, bisected, basically, by the two pack claims. Now, my grandson and his friend, James, were swimming one day and found some large chunks of gold, amethyst, and sapphire near the center of the lake. I reckon that all of it is worth probably close to twenty-thousand dollars, maybe more."

She paused, gratefully accepting the cup of tea that Camille deposited into her hands and taking a sip while Camille wandered back towards the front of the shop.

"I see," I said, filling the silence while she gathered her thoughts.

She smiled sadly at me and shook her head, setting her tea gently on the table between us.

"Now, since it was near the center of the lake, the other two boys, Andy and Chris, are claiming that it belongs to them. They were swimming in the lake that day when my boys found it, and claimed that they crossed the center boundary."

"So there's a dispute over which side of the lake the minerals were on, is that correct?"

She nodded, a sour look on her face.

"Well, in order to properly mediate this, I think I need to see the lake and where, exactly, the boys found the minerals. Do you think that's possible?"

"Of course, dear. Are you able to shift? I could take you there now, but it's quite a hike on two legs."

"I am. Let me just inform Camille and call Glenn."

"Of course, dear."

I gave Camille a brief rundown, quirking a brow at her wide smile.

"What's that look for?"

"I'm just so happy that you're taking the plunge. No pun intended."

"Of course not," I said, rolling my eyes. "I don't know when, or if, I'll be back today."

"Don't worry about me, Everly. Go do your thing, Watcher."

I grinned at her and grabbed my cell, dialing Glenn's number.

"Hey, Everly, what's up?"

"Hey Glenn. Remember how I told you I was going to start doing limited Watcher duties?"

"Like I could forget." I could practically hear the eyeroll in his voice.

"Well, I have my first mediation. It's about some precious minerals and stuff found in a lake that is on both Moon Walker and Shadow Keeper land. I was hoping you'd be willing to go with me to check it out."

"Of course. I'll be right over, give me five minutes to close up."

"Thanks, Glenn."

"Anything for you, Silver."

I was grinning at the phone like an idiot when I hung up. Camille quirked an eyebrow at me, but I just shrugged and went back to Miss Derin.

"Alright, Glenn will be here in a few minutes. He'll join us to check the lake. Will your grandson meet us there?"

"Yes, he will. Thank you so much for taking this on, Everly. I was really worried that the boys would end up starting a pack war over this."

"We won't let that happen."

She smiled and finished her tea, carrying the mug back to the café and depositing it on the counter. Glenn arrived moments later, waving at

Camille before escorting Miss Derin and me towards the edge of the forest behind the shops on the main strip of town.

"Alright, Ma'am, we'll follow your lead," he said before smoothly shifting into his oversized gray wolf.

In moments, we were racing through the forest behind the thin frame of Miss Derin's wolf. It took nearly half an hour to reach the lake in our four-legged bodies, so I could only imagine how long it would have taken on two feet, and not for the first time, I was grateful for Ghost Wolf's presence.

Once we broke from the trees, Miss Derin shifted. Glenn followed suit, but I remained in wolf form a little longer, sniffing around the lake. It was obvious, from the scents, where Shadow Keeper land began and Moon Walker ended. We broke through the trees close to the boundary, but the shaggy wolf we were meeting came from the heart of Moon Walker territory. He shifted and approached us, a frown on his face. I glanced at Glenn before shifting as well, and joining their little huddle.

"Alpha," he nodded respectfully at Glenn before facing his grandma.

"What did you want me to show you, Gram?"

She patted his cheek and steered him to face me.

"Brady, this is Everly. Everly, this is Brady. She's the new watcher, dear, and she's going to help you with your dispute."

He curled his lip and rolled his shoulders back. "I found those gems, and that gold, fair and square. Those Shadow Keeper scum have no claim to them."

I resisted the urge to roll my eyes and nodded.

"That may be so, but we have to be diplomatic here. If you were on the wrong side of the lake, they might have a claim. Show me where you found them, please."

He muttered something under his breath and stomped towards the lake, shifting seamlessly as he launched himself into the clear water. I quirked a brow at Glenn who grinned and waved me forward.

We followed the surly young man, shifting and paddling out towards the center of the lake where he let out a little yip before diving under. Under the water, he nosed a shallow outcropping of grainy rocks. It was riddled with holes, and I could see more glimmering metals and minerals trapped in their confines. I nodded towards the young man and surfaced just above the indicated rocks, glancing around. We were in the exact center of the lake. Naturally, my first mediation couldn't be a simple yes or no. I huffed and paddled back towards shore, shaking the water from my coat before shifting back.

His grandmother looked at me expectantly, but I just shook my head and grimaced, waiting for Glenn and Brady.

Once both men had shifted back, Brady glared at me.

"Well? It's mine, isn't it? Shadow Keeper has no claim."

I grimaced and shrugged.

"Unfortunately, it looks like they might, Brady. It was exactly in the center of the lake. Part of that outcropping is on the Moon Walker side, and part is on the Shadow Keeper side. If you took even a little bit from their side, they have a claim, according to pack laws."

He growled and stomped away.

"Brady, wait."

Glenn watched him with a frown.

"Brady!" I shouted, but he just sneered at me.

"Brady Camden, you will not ignore your Watcher," Glenn commanded, his voice laced with power, and the muscles strained in Brady's shoulders as he attempted to ignore his alpha.

"Brady," I said, my words softer but no less powerful than Glenn's, "We're going to work this out in a way that you don't lose what you worked for, but you need to listen to me. If you don't, then I can't promise your safety."

He turned towards me, fast as a whip, his eyes flashing.

"Are you threatening me, Watcher?"

"No. I'm telling you the facts. If you don't like my solution, and choose to act against me or those involved in this mediation, then I will have no choice but to submit you to the council. If they agree with my solution, which they will, since what I'm proposing makes sense, then your wolf will be bound and you'll be exiled from all Ley Bound counties. Is that really what you want?"

The fire leaked from his eyes as he deflated and shook his head.

"No, Watcher. I apologize."

I nodded and turned back towards the lake.

"Good. Now, we're going to carefully excavate the remaining mineral. Carefully, so as not to damage the rock, the lake, or anything else about the environment. Then, we're going to pool all of the minerals. Is your concern the value?"

"Yes, Watcher. It's enough to pay for my college tuition."

"Alright. Then what we'll do once we've excavated all of the minerals we can without damaging anything, is we'll get a valuation on everything, and then split it evenly between all four males involved in this dispute. It might be less than you're hoping, but it might be more. What really matters is that everyone should be happy with this solution, alright?"

He nodded, some of the anger fading from his eyes.

"Good. And if you don't have enough to pay for your college tuition, you come and talk to me, and we'll find you some work. Understand?"

His mouth popped open, but he quickly snapped it shut and nodded again, and when I turned back to Glenn, I found his eyes shining with approval.

Guess I hadn't totally screwed up, then.

CHAPTER NINE

We got to work right away, tugging bits of gems of varying shades and hues, as well as what looked like gold and silver from the little cache of treasure. I doubted very much that this was a natural deposit, but that wasn't relevant to the dispute, so I didn't mention it. The last thing they needed was something else to argue over.

The sun was setting by the time we had finished. We had quite the pile of sparkling monstrosities. Thankfully, Glenn had thought ahead, and had an empty canvas bag with him, in which we placed all the minerals. Brady promised to collect the remaining minerals and meet us back at my shop, where Glenn had arranged for someone who was more versed in gems and minerals to meet us and evaluate them. He also reached out to Hunter's dad, since Hunter himself was out of town, and got his agreement to come to the shop with the other two boys who were disputing Brady and James' claim.

We arrived back at the shop to find five new individuals who I hadn't yet met waiting, plus Brady.

Once everyone had been introduced, we made our way to the back seating area, where Camille had arranged a few more seats. Instead of four loungers, there were now eight and two tables. She grinned at me and mouthed 'Glenn' when I shot her a questioning look. I nodded and explained the situation and my proposed solution to everyone.

Hunter's dad grunted, but didn't otherwise protest. I got the feeling that he wasn't pleased, but it had nothing to do with my solution and everything to do with Glenn by my side. I decided to ignore his animosity until we had dealt with the situation at hand.

When all was said and done, our appraiser indicated that we had over $70,000 worth of gold, silver, tourmaline, sapphire, and amethyst. He suggested making sure each boy got an equal, or as near to equal as we could get, amount of each mineral. Everyone agreed, and waited, watching with greedy eyes, as the appraiser divided everything up.

"Now," he said, clapping his hands, "either you boys can hold onto this and take it wherever you want later to sell or convert to jewelry, or I can buy it from you to save you the hassle, or a mix of the two."

The boys managed to have a civil discussion with each other and the appraiser, ultimately deciding that they all wanted to keep a few pieces and sell the rest.

It was a relief when they all finally left, well past time for Camille and I to close up shop. Glenn smiled as he watched the young men saunter out of the shop, suddenly much more friendly than they had been when the day had begun.

"Disaster averted, Silver. Good job. That was one hell of a solution. Offering to find Brady work if his cut didn't add up to enough for his tuition? Smart thinking. Eustice would be proud."

I blushed at his words, turning away at the sound of a snort. Hunter's dad was still sitting in the back of the shop, watching me through narrowed eyes. Apparently, my solution didn't strike him as quite so genius.

I blew out a breath and squared my shoulders, then walked calmly across the room to him.

"Is there something amusing you, Elder Alpha Rowan?" I demanded haughtily.

He quirked an eyebrow, smirking as he looked me up and down.

"Ah, there's that fire that Eustice was known for. I almost thought you were a little pushover for a moment there. After all, why would a powerful Watcher choose Glenn over Hunter?"

Glenn snickered behind me as my mouth fell open in shock.

"Excuse me, but what the hell is that supposed to mean? I *didn't* choose Glenn over Hunter. And I didn't choose Hunter over Glenn. They're both my mates. And so is Blade, for that matter. Not that it's any of your damn business who I'm fated to, or what I choose to do about it."

He reeled back in shock, his mouth flapping much like a fish.

"They're...all you mates?" he choked out.

I glared at him, crossing my arms. "Damn straight."

"My gods. I...I didn't know."

I arched an eyebrow. "You mean you didn't know that Hunter had moved in with me this week? Along with Blade and Glenn? So that we can live together, as mates."

His brow furrowed and he glanced at Glenn, as if trying to work out if I was lying. Glenn nodded, and I pivoted on my heel and marched away. Bad enough I was getting shit from the council; I wasn't about to take it from the people in my own territory, and the father of the man I was fated to, at that.

"Wait, Everly. I'm sorry," the elder alpha said softly.

I spun back, surprised at the apology.

"Hunter doesn't tell me much. I just thought, that since Glenn was here with you and Hunter wasn't... since I was called in instead of him..."

I cut him off, slashing my hand through the air. "You were making assumptions that you had no right to make. Hunter is out of town on council business, or he would be here too. Blade would probably have come along as well to see how I handled things, but they've gone together."

Hunter's father looked shocked by my words.

"Blade and Hunter are working together?"

"They are. Now, if you'll excuse me, I'm quite tired and ready to close shop and head home."

He nodded, slinking out of the shop without another word while

Glenn and Camille watched me with matching looks of bemusement.

"What?" I grumbled. "He was being a Class A asshole."

We all burst out laughing, losing ourselves for a moment before closing the shop for the day.

Glenn and I headed home after waving goodbye to Camille, Glenn riding with me rather than grabbing his car.

"That was quite impressive for your first mediation, Everly."

"Thanks, Glenn. I was pretty nervous, but once I got going, it just made sense."

He nodded, a small smile on his face as we pulled up in front of the house. Hunter's truck was still gone.

"When are they supposed to be home? Is Blade back?" I couldn't help but notice his car was parked up there.

"No, believe it or not, they rode together. Don't worry, I'm sure they'll be home soon."

"Right."

We made our way inside in companionable silence. Glenn prepared a simple dinner: steak salad.

"I didn't picture you for the salad type of guy," I said with a chuckle.

He grinned and shrugged.

"I like lots of food in my human form. My wolf can have all the meat he wants, but I prefer some variety every now and then."

I snickered. "Tell that to Hunter. I swear he'd eat raw steak daily if we let him."

Glenn chuckled and nodded, watching me from the corner of his eye.

"What? Do I have something on my face?"

He smiled and shook his head.

"No. I'm just enjoying the view. You were amazing today, Everly. I was worried when you told me you wanted to start taking up your Watcher duties, but I can see now that there wasn't any point in worrying. You're a natural."

We lapsed into silence before a thought occurred to me.

"Glenn?"

"Hm?"

"When I first got here, there were envelopes of money in the shop. Were those payments for mediation and stuff?"

"Yep. I imagine that you'll be getting a chunk of the money the boys made from your solution. Eustice ran on an honor and what you can afford type of system. She never requested or expected payment, but was always pleasantly surprised when she got some. Most people pay something, and a few people pay a lot. It's rare that someone pays nothing, but when it happens it's usually in extreme circumstances."

"None of the envelopes were labeled with anything other than Grandma's name," I murmured, thinking back to the big basket of cash that I tripped over on my first day in the shop.

"Yeah. The only sign of who paid is usually the scent. That's how Eustice liked it, so nobody felt pressured to give more than they could afford."

"Huh. That makes sense."

"Eustice would offer her services for free, but most people didn't feel right taking so much of her time for nothing."

"Yeah, I guess I can see that. But it's just part of the job."

"And jobs tend to pay," he said with a smirk.

I rolled my eyes and finished eating, enjoying the quiet comradery and the not-meat centric meal.

*

The next morning I arrived at the shop a little later than I had planned after sleeping in. It was strange not waking early to train, but I felt more rested than I had in weeks, so I wasn't complaining.

"Hey Cam, any new requests?"

"Not yet, but I'm sure it's only a matter of time now that word is out."

"Wait, it is?"

She chuckled and tossed me the local paper. Right there, on the front page, was a picture of the shop.

'Everly Anderson, granddaughter of our beloved Eustice Cummings, is here in Wolf Lake and ready to work! She reopened Eustice's shop, Wolf Lake Books and Tea, a few months ago, but until yesterday, they weren't fully open. She's indicated that she's taking on limited duties while working her way back to the grandeur of Eustice's legacy. In other news, Everly is definitely the girl to watch, having snagged the hearts and souls of all three of Wolf Lake's most eligible bachelors. Watch out, ladies: Blade, Hunter, and Glenn all have their sights set on sharing the newest addition to Wolf Lake.'

The article went on about the services that Grandma used to offer in vague terms, while dropping hints about my mates living with me. I couldn't help the numerous eye rolls that worked their way out of me while I read.

"Great, just great. Now I'm going to have jealous exes and wannabe mistresses clawing around," I grumbled, making Camille burst out laughing.

I glared at her, but she was too busy having a hysterical meltdown to react. When she finally collected herself, wiping tears of mirth from her eyes, she grinned at me.

"Everly, you don't need to worry. Nobody is going to mess with your men. Nobody wants to fuck with someone's mate."

"But it didn't say we were mates, just that they're all chasing my tail!"

She giggled again, shaking her head.

"We can't exactly print 'New Watcher is super powerful wolf shifter with three mates.' What if an outsider got ahold of the paper?"

My brow furrowed as I realized that she was right. The paper always spoke about supernatural and shifter business in such a roundabout way that someone who wasn't familiar with any of it wouldn't be suspicious, not really. I was so new to the world of supernatural phenomenon, that I hadn't even noticed how vague the articles usually were. I couldn't help but wonder if it was the same elsewhere. Did the articles back home have some hidden meaning?

When the first customer of the day came in, searching for a newly released fantasy book, I got lost in my work, pushing my worries and wonderings to the side to focus on the tasks at hand.

We had more customers come in than usual, but most of them weren't interested in books, they just wanted to meet me, shake my hand, learn about how I was settling in and how I liked everything so far. It was like, with my actions from yesterday, I had unlocked some hidden barrier that kept people hidden from me—or me hidden from them. People came in to meet me, learn how I was settling in, and then bought a tea or pastry before heading out.

Camille and I settled into a routine with the shop busier than ever. No more requests came in, but people were eager to speak with me throughout the week. The Oberon were mentioned once or twice, but no expectations were placed on me, much to my relief. Blade and Hunter finally came home about half-way through the week. At first, they were upset that I had accepted a Watcher contract, but after Glenn explained how I handled everything, they agreed that it was the right move. Which was good, because if they'd tried to send me home to play the meek little mate after the amateur heroics they'd run off to attempt behind my back, I'd have made them both sleep in the basement.

Things went back to normal, or as normal as life can be for a wolf shifter who's on the chopping block with the council. Hunter trained me, teaching me physical combat techniques, how to fight and shift quickly, how to channel my wolf's strength and senses when in human form, and so much more that I hope I never need for survival. Glenn taught me about my innate magic, and how to use and channel it, while Blade continued to focus on the knowledge I would need to do my duties as Watcher and to face the council.

Life wasn't exactly peaceful, but it was predictable, and I liked that.

I should have known better than to get too comfortable.

"As you know, since the article in the tribune, I've been getting lots of questions about you, Everly," Blade said nonchalantly during our Saturday night family dinner.

I nodded absently, twirling my spaghetti.

"Yeah, the pack won't shut up about how amazing you are. Lots of people have been buying books they don't want or need just to get a chance to look at and talk to you," Hunter said with a bemused smirk.

I rolled my eyes, glancing at Glenn. He nodded at my silent question, confirming that he was getting harassed as well.

When I'd read that article, I was afraid that something like this might happen, but I'd had my head buried in the sand while we went about our lives.

"You know, we only have a little over a month before the council meeting," Blade said seriously once his plate was cleared.

I choked on my water at his words. I knew we didn't have that long to prepare to begin with, but having it put into such plain words was shocking.

Hunter slapped my back, waiting for me to catch my breath before speaking.

"I think it's time you met the packs, Everly."

"I've already met them," I muttered, avoiding his gaze.

Glenn snickered, and my eyes snapped up to meet his.

"Having random people come by your shop to feel you out doesn't count as meeting the packs, Silver. You need to meet the whole pack, chat with them, play games, attend a meeting... Join a run."

Every word had my stomach twisting. I wasn't afraid of meeting new people, but meeting a whole pack of, what, like fifty people, or more? At once? I was pretty sure I'd rather face down the Oberon.

"Why can't you just keep having them come to the shop?" I asked, because apparently I was an optimist.

Blade shook his head.

"That's not enough and you know it, Everly. You need to make friends—allies—in the packs. All three of them. Having just one or two people who like and support you means that the council only has to deal with one or two people to get rid of you. Having whole packs that like and support you? That's harder to cover up."

I ground my teeth together. Blade was right, of course. He was always right, but I didn't feel like I was ready.

Treoirn snorted in my head.

What was that for, Ghostie?

I told you not to call me Ghostie, she growled.

I snickered and glanced at the mirror on the wall, watching as my eyes flashed.

You need to meet your mates' packs. We will never be beholden to a pack, but making allies is always a good idea, Gaelana.

Right.

I glanced at my mates, who were watching me expectantly, and blew out a stream of air.

"Alright. When?"

Hunter grinned and glanced at Blade, who nodded in agreement to some unspoken conversation. It was nice that they seemed to be getting along, but somewhat less so when they used their newfound friendship to corner me like this.

"We'll start this week. You can skip your evening training in favor of attending the pack meetings."

"Wait, all three packs?"

"Yes. The sooner the better. It's probably best for you to attend at least two pack meetings before the summit, for each pack, plus continue making nice with people who come to the shop."

"Right," I said with a grimace.

At least these shifters wouldn't be trying to kill me.

Probably.

CHAPTER TEN

You'd think that agreeing to meet hundreds of strangers in the coming days would be a solid reason for lightening my workload, but it turned out that my mates felt differently.

When I awoke to train with Hunter the next morning, I was greeted by the grinning faces of Blade and Glenn as well, both of them in workout gear. I narrowed my eyes, glaring at them as we ate, but they remained silent.

When I trudged outside to join Hunter, both Glenn and Blade were hot on my heels, an anticipation in their every move that filled me with dread.

Whatever my mates had planned this morning, I had a feeling that I was not going to like it.

Glenn and Blade overtook me, moving to stand beside Hunter and whisper in low enough voices that I couldn't make out their words, even when channeling my wolf.

Annoyed, I began stretching, getting distracted when each of them started to stretch as well, bending over and showing me their delicious rear ends. Treoirn's attention snagged there, too, and I could feel her primal need to claim our mates. Claim *all* of our mates. I was starting to think she had a point.

Hunter's shorts were relatively loose, but Blade was wearing bike shorts that hugged his ass perfectly, leaving little to the imagination when he bent over to touch his toes. My mouth watered at the sight of the bulge between his legs. I wanted to run my tongue over every inch of that firm flesh.

Glenn's chuckle snapped me from my mesmerized gaze to find him shirtless, just a pair of basketball shorts hung low on his hip. I moaned as

I leaned forward to stretch out my other leg. He was perfect, his defined muscles rippling deliciously in the early morning light.

These men were going to be the death of me. I had gotten used to ignoring the way Hunter's body flexed, gotten accustomed to pretending I didn't want to jump him every second of every training session, but I didn't have the same practice at ignoring a half-naked Glenn and Blade, and I knew that lack of discipline was going to cost me today. Still, my body began to hum with anticipation at the nearness of my mates, thoughts of all the things I wish we were doing right now instead flitting through my mind.

"Earth to Everly," Hunter's amused tone snapped me from my thirsty musings.

I rolled my eyes and ducked my head to pull my hair into a ponytail in an attempt to hide my flaming cheeks, but judging by his chuckle, I failed.

"Why are they here?" I asked when the heat had died down a little.

Hunter smirked and crossed his arms, staring at me until I met his eyes. The fire in them had me flinching.

"Today, little mate, we're going to see how you react when you're outnumbered," he purred.

A groan escaped me before I could stop it.

Blade huffed and stomped over.

"None of that, Everly. We need to make sure you can take care of yourself when we're not around. It's obvious that the Oberon are targeting you, and now the council is as well. We can't trust anyone to play fair, so you need to be able to kick their asses no matter how outnumbered you are."

I blew out a breath. Blade was right, as always. I was starting to get irritated by that tendency, but rather than sass him, I just nodded and marched forward.

I waited for instructions, but for once, they didn't come. Instead, all three men stalked towards me, dark looks in their eyes. These were my mates, I knew, but the look in their eyes scared me even so.

It's just training, Everly, calm down, I told myself firmly.

But I couldn't calm down when they moved like that. Like predators. And I was their prey. I backed up slowly, inching towards the open space between my house and the forest, trying not to shake at the dark glint in their eyes. For a moment, I was worried that the Oberon had gotten to them, but I could feel Hunter through our mate bond, and there wasn't any of the darkness I associated with the Oberon in him.

This was training, and my mates were intent on making sure I took it seriously, even if they had to scare me to do it.

And that pissed me the hell off.

How dare they try to scare me? How dare they! I shuddered with rage as Hunter darted forward.

I was shaking so badly that I almost didn't move in time, but I managed to avoid his strike. He nodded, falling back while Blade and Glenn moved closer. I could see their wolves in their eyes, just below the surface, snarling. I couldn't tell if the anger in their wolves was at them, or at me, but I didn't want to find out, so I fell down into one of the fighting stances Hunter had shown me. It was one of the first we had gone over, with my weight evenly dispersed on the balls of my feet, my legs positioned so I could move in almost any direction within fractions of a second.

Glenn moved towards me next, and he was fast, faster than Hunter, but I managed to twirl away before he could grab me. Before I could regain my balance, however, Blade was there, his fist whipping out towards my face. In the back of my mind, I was reeling in shock, but my body moved almost of its own accord, my arm darting up and pushing his fist to the side before I twisted and side stepped, coming face to face with Hunter once more.

He was grinning, a proud glint in his eye that reassured me of this being more test than anything else. Still, that anger was there inside of me, simmering just under the surface. The indignity of them never keeping me in the loop, making plans for me, going off and doing things to protect me without consulting me.

I had been brushing it aside, wanting to avoid conflict with the men who were so important to me, but being blindsided, first last night by their demand that I meet the packs, and then this morning by their insistence that I learn to fight multiple opponents, had me boiling with repressed rage.

They have no right to make decisions for me without even asking my opinion, I growled within my mind as Hunter struck out at me.

I ducked his blow and lashed out with one of my own, just barely grazing his side as he jumped back. Then Glenn and Blade were on me again, working together to herd me back towards the house as I mentally fumed.

How dared they try to control my life? Did they think that, just because we're mates, they had a right to treat me as less than them?

I lashed out at Glenn, catching him in the solar plexus and sending him stumbling backwards while ducking another blow from Blade, Hunter stalking up, trying to circle behind me.

It was about damned time they learned that we were equals. If they wanted to be with me, then they would damn well accept that I would have a seat at the decision-making table. I was their mate, not their pet.

Yes! Rage, Gaelana! Treoirn howling in my mind as my tirade continued.

Blade rushed me, trying to catch me in a football tackle, but I sidestepped him again, bringing my elbow down on the back of his neck with most of the suppressed rage I'd been carrying within me since coming to Wolf Lake. I pulled my blow just enough to ensure I didn't do any lasting damage. He was my mate, after all. I wanted his respect, not his death.

As he went down, Hunter grabbed me from behind, trapping my arms against my side and awakening a whole new vat of anger. One of my mother's scummy boyfriends grabbed me like this once.

I went lax, loosening all of my muscles and dropping my weight so that Hunter was supporting me. He stumbled back, startled, and I slid down to the ground, out of his arms, and lashed out with my leg, sweeping it across his ankles and dropping him to the ground just as Glenn recovered and came at me again, whooping with joy.

The sound gave me pause, rattling some of my anger free.

This is just training, Everly, I reminded myself.

Still, training or not, I needed to show these boys who was the boss around here, because they seemed to think it was them, and it definitely was not.

As Glenn rushed me in a similar manner to the way Blade came at me, I steadied myself, dropping my shoulder and loosening some of my muscles, ready to absorb the blow. We collided, and I rolled with the impact, bringing my shoulder down and into his stomach, which was rock hard, and flipping him over my shoulder, using his own momentum against him.

He hit the ground hard, hissing in pain.

Hunter was pulling himself up, dusting the grass off his pants without a care in the world, while I readied for another round. Instead of rushing me again, however, he shot me a breathtaking grin that left me floundering, all my anger leaking out of me.

Blade groaned as Glenn helped him to his feet, Glenn cackling happily.

"You did great, little mate."

"That was something else, Everly. It was like you flipped a switch from sweet and sexy to badass and ready to kill. Good. You'll need whatever the hell you just tapped into," Blade said, rubbing the back of his neck where my elbow connected.

I looked down, somewhat embarrassed by how hard I hit him.

"Now that we know you can handle yourself in human form without using magic, let's work on a few other things. I want you to be able to take out five opponents who are stronger than you in human and wolf form, with and without your magic. You might be in a position one day where you can't access your magic for whatever reason, or your wolf, so you need to be able to take out a stronger, faster, and more powerful opponent even when you don't have access to your wolf and your magic."

I frowned at Hunter. I understood his logic, but this went deeper than just fear for my safety or worry over the Oberon. He was acting like me being attacked and being outmatched was inevitable. Whatever he and Blade found while they were gone must've been serious.

Which meant they were keeping things from me. Again. I squared my leg and crossed my arms, ready to go to battle with my own mates for my place in this world.

"What aren't you telling me, Hunter?" I demanded, startling him.

He blinked at me like he wasn't expecting a response at all, glancing at Blade. I growled at their look.

"No, don't look at Blade for help. What the fuck are you assholes hiding?"

Blade looked confused, but Glenn stepped back, having already been subjected to one of my tirades.

"What do you mean, Everly?" Blade asked, a frown marring his perfect face.

Do not let the sexy mates distract you, Everly!

I gritted my teeth and marched up to where Blade and Hunter were standing, side by side while Glenn snuck further away, taking up a seat on the edge of the porch to watch the inevitable fallout.

"What I mean, Blade, is that you and Hunter are hiding shit from me. You didn't tell me you were going out of town to investigate the council. You didn't tell me that you had made arrangements for me to meet your packs— Yes, I know that you already made the plans. Hunter didn't tell me that I was the only one who could harm or cleanse the Oberon. You haven't told me what you found when you went out of town."

Blade's frown deepened with every item I listed. Hunter crossed his arms, a mulish set to his face.

I glared at Hunter and poked his chest.

"Just because you're the big, bad alphas, doesn't mean you get to make my decisions for me. I am an adult. I am the Watcher. I'm supposed to be your mate, not your bitch."

Blade flinched at the venom in my tone, shrinking a little as though, for the first time in his life, he was questioning his actions.

"You're not, Everly, that's not what we—"

I slashed my hand in the air, cutting him off.

"You are treating me like a child, Blade. You're hiding things from me, making decisions for me, and pushing me to learn things without ever giving me an explanation about why, or a chance to actually put the knowledge into practice. Yes, I'm your mate, and yes, I get that you want to protect me, but you can't wrap me in bubble wrap and place me in a corner."

Hunter opened his mouth to protest, but snapped it shut abruptly when I glared at him.

"Remember, *I'm* the one with three mates. *I'm* the one with the power to fix the Oberon mess. *I'm* the one who is being summoned to the council."

Blade grimaced and Hunter uncrossed his arms, a contrite look on his face.

"Everything I've learned since I've come here points to me needing to be willing, able, and ready to fight the Oberon and solve problems and stand against this threat, and to do that, I need to know what I'm facing. I need to know that you guys have my back, and that you're not going to hold me back because of some misplaced sense of, I don't know, male protectiveness. I'm stronger than you think. I can handle whatever is thrown at me, but if you keep using kid gloves with me, then I won't be ready. And I sure as hell won't still be here. Stop hiding things from me and making decisions for me, and start treating me like I deserve the same kind of respect you would give my grandma."

They both had the decency to look ashamed, but it was Blade who nodded and grabbed my hand.

"You're right, Everly. We've been keeping things from you and making decisions for and about you without your input. That was wrong of us."

I pulled my hand back after he planted a kiss on my knuckles, crossing my arms and trying to hold onto the anger that was quickly fizzling out.

"Glenn warned us that you wouldn't like to be kept out of the loop like this," Hunter admitted, glancing over his shoulder to catch Glenn's eye. They nodded at each other, and then Glenn joined us out on the lawn.

"We'll tell you everything, Everly, but it's not going to be quick."

"I'll show you what I've found when I pick you up for tonight's pack run," Blade murmured, slinking back into the house.

I watched him go, longing to call him back, but I knew he needed time to process just how badly he'd fucked up and how to fix it, so I turn to face Glenn and Hunter instead. Hunter got right into his explanation about how he and Blade found evidence of several council members being compromised, but they couldn't tell if they were compromised by the Oberon or some other threat, and that was why they want to ensure that I could handle myself in any situation.

    I understood their concern, and told Hunter as much, and he agreed to do more to keep me in the loop, and to stop making decisions for me without consulting me first. I counted it as a win, so when he made his excuses to cut the rest of our morning short, I didn't protest, instead racing upstairs to enjoy a nice, long shower before heading to the shop.

CHAPTER ELEVEN

I was just getting ready to leave for lunch when a stranger entered the shop. Something about him seemed off. There was an aura of danger around him that made me cautious, even nauseous, but rather than let on that I was affected, I greeted him cheerfully.

"Hello! Welcome to Wolf Lake Books and Tea, can I help you find anything?"

The man stared at me as if he was looking through my soul, a slight frown on his face. I looked around, wondering where Camille had gotten off to, but didn't see her anywhere. Great. Just my luck.

I didn't get the feeling that I should turn my back on this person, so when he didn't respond for a moment, I just stood there with a dumb smile on my face.

He scowled at me before shaking his head and glancing around.

"You're Gaelana?" he demanded in a rough voice that sent chills down my spine.

Treoirn, how does he know that name? Is it common knowledge?

I could feel the frown in her voice when she replied.

No, it's not, Gaelana. Tread carefully with this one.

I straightened my spine and stared into the stranger's eyes, hoping to find some clue as to who he was and what he wanted.

"Generally, you introduce yourself to someone before demanding knowledge of their heritage," I said airily, trying to appear unaffected, and probably not being quite as convincing as I'd have liked.

The stranger smirked and shook his head.

"Apologies, Miss. My name is Orin."

"Everly," I said mildly, taking a risk and turning my back on him to retreat to the main desk.

He chuckled and followed behind me, close enough that I could feel the heat of him. It didn't leave me all warm and fuzzy like when I felt my mates so close behind me.

I moved behind the desk and took a seat, turning to glance at Orin dismissively.

"How can I help you, Orin?"

He smiled at me, the expression softening his sharp features just enough to make me a little less wary.

"I'm actually here because I believe I can help you," he purred, leaning against the desk.

"Oh? And how would that be?"

"Well," he said, trailing his fingers along the desk and leaving a glowing trail of magic that had my eyes narrowing. "I believe I can shed some light on the scourge that is plaguing your kind. I believe you refer to it as the Oberon, no?"

I narrowed my eyes at him, not sure I should believe his words, but desperate for more information about the diseased darkness that had been stalking my new home.

"I'm listening," I said simply.

The door swung open behind us and Camille stepped from the restroom, gasping before she fixed her face into a glare at Orin. He narrowed his eyes at her before glancing back to me.

"Not here," he said simply, slipping a card across the desk and disappearing out the door.

That was...odd, I think, reaching for Treoirn.

Yes, it was, Gaelana. You should reach out to him.

Why did he look at Camille like that?

I cannot say, but perhaps the information he offers can help us to end this war.

I nodded, slipping the card off the desk and into my packet as Camille approached. Something about his reaction to her—and hers to him—left me uneasy, and I found myself not wanting her to know about the card, which had me worried about my own reactions. Grandma told me to trust my instincts, though, and they were screaming at me to hide the card before Camille saw it, so I did.

"Who was that?" she asked as I vacated her chair.

"I don't know," I admitted, glancing at the door. "But he was weird."

She nodded, adjusting in her chair.

"The fae usually are. They're dangerous, too. You should stay away from him."

"Oh? He was fae?"

She nodded.

"Why are they dangerous?"

"The fae never do anything without a reason. There's always something in it for them, a bargain, a deal. They can't be trusted."

"Good to know. So if I ever run into a fae who offers information?"

"Be wary about accepting it, or trusting it. Fae can't tell an outright lie, but they are masters at twisting words and manipulating meanings. If a fae ever offers you free information, whatever they expect you to do with it is likely going to benefit them more than you."

"Good to know."

She nodded again, picking up the book she'd been reading between customers and burying her nose in the pages.

"I'll see you later, Cam. I have to grab something to eat before I meet Blade for whatever he needs to tell me before the pack run."

"Sure thing, boss."

Once I was out of the shop and down the street, I was able to breathe a little easier. Something about the way Camille and the stranger stared at each other had me on edge, and I couldn't understand why, but I knew I needed to talk to him again. I pulled the card out and dialed the number on the back. When the stranger answered, the card dissolved in my hand—which was more than a little creepy.

"Everly. I knew you'd call."

"What did you want to tell me?"

"It's not safe to speak in this manner, I'm afraid. It would be best if I wasn't seen interacting with you again, for your own safety. My presence may have put more of a target on your back."

His words gave me pause. I don't know why, but I got the sense that he was worried for me. Then again, given what Camille had said, if he was worried for my safety, it was properly because he wanted me alive and able to do something for him. But what could I do that a fae, clearly with some powerful magic, couldn't?

"What did you have in mind?" I asked, my thoughts buzzing with puzzle pieces that didn't quite fit.

"Can you get away to Denver for an afternoon without drawing suspicion?"

I thought about it for a moment, but decided that I really needed to meet with Orin. Whatever he had to tell me was important, I knew that much.

"Yeah. I could probably get out on Tuesday. I'll tell my mates that I'm meeting an old friend from Oregon."

"Alright. You could probably let them know that you're meeting me, if you've bonded, but I wouldn't advise telling anyone else."

"Noted."

"I'll text you the address of a restaurant we can meet at. Supernaturals only, and sound wards in place to avoid prying ears."

"Very well. Morning or early afternoon works best for me."

I had a date that evening with one of my gorgeous mates, and blowing him off for Orin did not appeal in the slightest.

"I'll make the arrangements. Does one p.m. work?"

"Yes, that's fine."

"I'll see you then. Don't save my number as Orin."

"Right." I rolled my eyes. Like the disappearing card hadn't been a clue on that front.

I hung up the phone and stored his number as Puck. His caution left me unsettled, but I also had this feeling that it was warranted. Necessary, even.

I shook the worries from my mind and grabbed a sub from down the street before heading towards the library. Blade was going to be driving me to his packlands, so there wasn't much point in driving the half mile to the library from my shop.

I sat outside the library, enjoying the feel of the sun playing across my face as I ate my lunch. My mind was whirring with information. Hunter and Blade suspected enough people on the council of being compromised that we couldn't be sure how the vote would fall, so I needed to be prepared, and I only had a month to do that.

I couldn't work out how they thought people were compromised, though. Did they think they were working with the Oberon? Did they believe that they wanted me gone, or were being blackmailed to vote a certain way? Whatever the cause for their potential to be compromised, we needed more information, and I had a feeling that Orin had some of what we needed.

He said that I could tell my mates if I was bonded to them, but I had only sealed the bond with Hunter. Did that mean that I couldn't tell Blade? Or Glenn? Why was Orin worried about that?

I was so lost in thought that I didn't notice Blade until he was standing right in front of me, hand on his hip, and watching me with a concerned look.

"What?" I asked, chewing the last bite of my food.

"You look worried."

"I am. There's a lot going on, and a lot riding on me learning as much as I can, as fast as I can."

His eyes softened as he nodded in agreement.

"Let's get to work. We'll focus on my pack today, and the who's who of it all. You won't be expected to know who everyone is, but it will help you when finding your place in the pack."

"Uh, but I'm not joining your pack…"

"No, but you'll be running with us, that means you'll have to earn your spot. You don't just get to run with the alpha because we're supposed to be mates, especially since we haven't bonded yet."

"Oh. That makes sense."

We spent the rest of the afternoon going over who Blade's beta was, how to recognize someone's natural rank, how to avoid starting fights with the more aggressive pack members, and how I should assert myself to ensure that I wasn't relegated to the outskirts of the run. Blade didn't seem surprised that I picked everything up quickly, but I was. It wasn't like I had any experience with this kind of thing.

By the time we arrived at Blade's packhouse, I was riddled with tension, and ready to get this whole thing over with.

The sun was setting when we pulled up to what I could only describe as a mansion with tons of outbuildings. Blade called it a packhouse, but I didn't think that term was sufficient. He admitted that there were over twenty-five rooms in the main house, and just as many between all of the outbuildings.

His pack had grown to be the largest in the region, with over a hundred and fifty members of all ages. Hunter's pack, he told me, was the next largest, and the oldest, with a little over a hundred members, many of whom could trace their lineage back to the first shifters. Then there was Glenn's pack, and with around ninety members, it wasn't small, but being a pack associated with gray magic, their numbers tended to be lower. Most shifters, I learned, leaned more towards light or dark magic.

I was confused, at first, about the different magics, but Blade assured me that it didn't mean someone was good or evil, just that their magic leaned more towards light or dark tendencies. Many Shadow Keeper wolves could move through shadows in a manner similar to vampires, and many Ghost Dancer wolves had the ability to bend light to some extent, allowing them to hide in plain sight.

When I'd asked Blade why they couldn't use those skills to fight the Oberon, he told me that they could bend light, but not control it.

Then there were the Moon Walker wolves. Their magic was gray magic, straddling the boundary between light and dark. Light magic was stronger during the day, dark magic at night, and then gray magic thrived in the between. Dusk, dawn, midnight, noon. Those were the times that gray wolves were strongest. It was fascinating to me, and made me curious as to what I'd be classified as. I was a little disappointed when Blade told me that I didn't fall into any one group, which is why my lineage claimed the title of Watcher. We were neutral, having a little bit of every type of magic. That meant we didn't have a specific time when we were stronger, but we also didn't have a time when we were weaker, either, which was something of a relief.

Blade introduced me to his pack in a whirlwind of faces and names that I had already tried, and failed, to memorize. Many of the wolves tried to have a staring contest with me, trying to force me to drop my gaze before them, but none of them had the strength in them to match me for more than a few seconds, much to my relief. Blade was amused, but I was curious more than anything.

Nothing really eventful happened, until he introduced me to his parents. His father was a large, intimidating man dressed like a New York stockbroker, and his mother was a timeless beauty in a designer sundress that probably cost more than my whole house. I didn't expect either to try and push their will on me, but both did, which made me got my back up.

Before I could say or do anything to put them in their places—or get my ass kicked, possibly—they both laughed, delighted by my lack of reaction to their challenges.

"Oh, she is a strong one, dear, no wonder she has three mates. I could feel her before you even pulled up."

Blade rolled his eyes, pulling his mother into a hug while his father smirked.

"You'll make a good Watcher, Everly Anderson," he said, his gravelly voice carrying despite his soft tone.

When it was time for the run, I ended up at Blade's side, much to my relief. He said that by not flinching from his parents' gazes, I had asserted that I was the strongest wolf here, and would be honored with the lead spot during the run. When I whispered to Blade that I didn't want to lead, he chuckled and promised to remain at my side, showing a united front to his wolves.

"Besides, it will show that you don't hold yourself above your mates. That will go a long way to winning you allies," he whispered back against my hair just before shifting.

I rolled my eyes and shifted, prancing up beside him and smacking him repeatedly with my tail while we waited for everyone else to shift.

Once everyone was ready, Blade's father loped up to us, circling us before yipping and falling back, just behind where we stood. Blade dipped his head at the elder alpha before pawing the ground and tilting his head back, releasing a haunting howl that left me shivering in anticipation.

The wolves behind us shifted restlessly as Blade nudged me, waiting for my howl to join his. When I tilted my head back and released a long, low howl, the rest of the pack behind us joined in, sending a shiver of power racing through me.

This was what it meant to run with a pack, this shiver of anticipation, the excitement, the raw power. Blade leaned into me, sharing more of that spark, letting me feel the pack through him.

Once we bond with him, you will feel them more closely. You will not be bound to any one pack, but you will have access to the strength of them all. That is what it means to have three alpha mates, Gaelana.

I was lost to the power racing through me, drunk on the need to run and hunt with the pack. Blade released a yip that drew me back to myself just enough to race forward, leading the hunt. He was by my side the whole night, pounding and stalking and playing as we howled at the moon and pranced through the forest with over a hundred wolves on our tails.

This was what it meant to be pack.

CHAPTER TWELVE

Monday morning came around far too soon after the late night with the Ghost Dancer pack, but despite my bone-deep exhaustion, I was downstairs and ready to train before the clock struck seven.

Once again, all three of my mates were present, but rather than their ambush tactics from the day before, they were much more relaxed—small mercies.

"Now that we know you can handle yourself in an unexpected situation, we're going to combine some of the things we've all been teaching you today," Hunter said simply, dragging some straw dummies to the center of the gravel area in front of the house.

I noticed that they had moved the cars well away from where they were setting everything up, which made me think we'd be playing with fire today.

While Hunter moved the dummies around, Blade approached me with a small smile.

"Do you recall our lessons about the different supernaturals and their weaknesses, Everly?"

"Yeah. Vampires, fae, shifters, demons, witches, warlocks, druids, sorcerers... Uhm, am I forgetting anything?"

"Good. Those are the primary archetypes. Each one can be further broken down, but we're going over generalities here on the most common weaknesses of each to ensure that we get the most impact in your training."

"Alright. So what's the plan?"

"Well, first, can you tell me the most common weakness of each?"

"Fae is iron, vampires are weak to white ash, sunrays for the younger ones, and fire; shifters tend to be weak against pure silver and wolf's bane, demons are vulnerable to birch, rowan, ash, alder, willow, hawthorn, and oak weapons that have been bathed in holy water and blessed on hallowed ground, witches and warlocks are vulnerable to white gold chains; druids are vulnerable to flame, and sorcerers are vulnerable when parted from any vessels containing magic."

"Good. There are more nuances, but that's the basics. Now, you won't always have a cursed blade on you, but you will always have access to your magic unless it's been bound. Today we're going to practice under the assumption that your magic is free and you have your full faculties about you. Hunter was able to enlist the help of a witch to give each of these mannequins the resistance of one of the main archetypes of paranormal. Your job today is to destroy them, using whatever you have at your disposal, as you stand here. Magic, claws, fists, whatever you have."

I frowned and inspected the mannequins. The task seemed simple, but my knowledge was limited. Glenn stepped up behind me and began massaging my shoulders while Hunter finished arranging the mannequins in a large circle.

"Alright, little mate. Blade briefed you on the assignment of the day. Today, nothing is fighting back, you just need to figure out how to eliminate them. When we resume on Wednesday, depending upon how far you get today, we'll probably start with some things hitting back. Thursday and Saturday we'll go back to group attacks and phase into working with a team. Next week, after you've run with all the packs, we'll start on group combat in mixed teams of shifted and non shifted fighter. We'll enlist the help of some pack members for that."

Well, that just sounded like a barrel of laughs. My mind was spinning just thinking about. Things were moving so quickly. They expected so much from me, and I wasn't sure that I could handle it.

Breathe, Gaelana. You'll be fine. Channel that rage you had yesterday. Rage won't always be the answer, but while you practice, it can teach you where your power resides. The more you practice, the easier it will be to call on your strength.

Treoirn's words calmed me enough for me to push the future to the back of my mind and just focus on the present.

We spent nearly three hours outside, with me hurling magic, claws, and fists at the dummies. I managed to eliminate the vampire, the shifter, the witch, the warlock, and the druid by the time we had finished. The demon, fae, and sorcerer were giving me trouble, though.

"Alright, little mate, that's enough for today. It's after ten already. You're exhausted. We're not going to break through the others today."

I growled at the demon mannequin. I knew I could take it out, I was just missing something.

Glenn chuckled and tugged me back, rubbing my shoulders again.

"Calm down, Silver. It's okay. Come, let me help you upstairs."

I reluctantly let him lead me away while Blade and Hunter cleaned up, discussing my progress in hushed tones.

"What am I missing, Glenn? I know it's something simple, something that should be obvious."

He smiled and steered me up the stairs and into my room, where he drew a bath while I glared at my dirty, sweaty reflection in the mirror.

"Well, now that the first day of this is done, I can help you out. Hunter wanted you to try without any extra hints today."

"Of course he did," I grumbled, much to Glenn's amusement.

"Think about it, Silver. If you're attacked when you're alone, we won't be there to give you hint about how to win the fight."

I deflated, nodding in agreement. Glenn chuckled and turned the shower on, testing the water before waving me over.

"We'll work on them more tomorrow. You're still having breakfast with me and doing a lesson on magic, right?"

"Yep."

"Good, then we'll focus on how to source your fire and light from different realms. I do the same with my water, so it will be easier for me to show you than one of the others."

I was so lost in thought that I didn't even notice when Glenn tugged my shirt off, just obediently lifted my arms for him while contemplating the possibilities. When he helped me step out of my pants, the feel of his strong hands gently stroking down my thighs snapped my attention back to reality.

I glanced down to find him admiring my legs, rubbing the sore muscles as he leisurely pulled my workout shorts down. A moan escaped me, drawing his attention back to my face.

He grinned and leaned forward, kissing the front of my thighs before steadying me so I could step out of the sweaty fabric.

"Glenn," I moaned, reaching down to run my fingers through his hair.

His eyes flashed, his wolf just below the surface, rumbling with pleasure. I could feel the alpha beast's desire, beating through Glenn. Treoirn sent an echoing pulse of desire racing through me, sending a thrill that heightened my own need shooting straight to my core. Glenn leaned forward and sniffed, releasing a strangled groan before stiffly rising to his feet.

"You make me crazy, Silver," he murmured before capturing my lips.

The kiss was hot and hard, more demanding than any of our previous kisses. I wanted more, and I wanted it now, so when Glenn pulled back, I growled, yanking his mouth back down while he chuckled in amusement.

He let me ravage his mouth, molding his lips to my own. He mirrored my every move, his desire an echo of my own. When I reached down and grasped his ass, tugging him closer, he groaned and pulled back again.

We were both panting, but when I tried to pull his mouth towards me again, he smiled softly and laid his forehead against my own. I could feel my frustration morph into a frown at what felt like rejection, but the way he still held me assuaged any hurt feelings. He wanted me, I knew he did.

"I wish we could finish this right now, Silver," he said, kissing the tip of my nose, "but I have to go with Blade to prepare some things for the Lodge. We're hoping to have a few meeting in the coming weeks there so the packs get accustomed to you having your own place to call meetings."

I sighed and nodded. Blade had told me about their plans before the run last night, but I had forgotten all about them in the bustle of activity this morning, and under the heat of Glenn's touch.

"I understand, Glenn. Thank you for taking care of me, mate."

He smiled and gave me one more sweet kiss before slipping out of the room on silent feet.

I groaned and hopped in the shower to wash off all the grime before enjoying the steaming bath, which Glenn had loaded with one of my favorite lavender Epson salts and set a glittery bath bomb on the edge of the tub. He really was an amazing mate.

I was a prune by the time Hunter came upstairs to collect me a couple of hours later. The water had long since grown tepid, but I was too relaxed to move.

Hunter took one look at me, lounging in the tub with one leg thrown over the side, and growled.

"Little mate, if we didn't have places to be, I would spend the rest of the day showing you just how delectable you are."

The growl in his voice sent heat racing straight to my core for the second time today, and I was tempted to beg him to cancel our plans. Unfortunately, he was the alpha apparent of the Shadow Keeper pack, and asking him to skip pack functions would be a low blow. I didn't doubt that he would if I asked, he was that type of man, but I could never be that selfish, no matter the temptation…and he was so very tempting. I didn't want to make him choose between me and his pack, so instead of begging for his hands to be on my body, I lifted myself out of the tub, enjoying the sight of his eyes roving over my body as the water dripped down, and stepped out of the tub.

"If we didn't have things to do," I purred, stalking towards him, "then I'd ask you to take me right now."

I reached up and tugged his head down, burying my hand in his hair, and kissed him with all the pent up passion inside of me. It was me who pulled back this time, leaving him groaning and adjusting his pants while I stalked to my closet to get ready for another afternoon of meeting shifters and proving that I deserve my place through petty dominance challenges.

I emerged less than ten minutes later, clothed in black leather pants that hugged my ass nicely and a studded crop top. Camille reluctantly told me that it was best to match my mate's aesthetic on the first pack meetings, and I agreed. Besides, this outfit made me look way more badass than I usually felt.

Hunter's eyes widened when he saw me, another possessive growl tearing itself from his throat and making me chuckle.

"Let's go, mate. It's time to meet the Shadow Keepers."

He drove, since my car was still at the shop from yesterday. We rode in a companionable silence, the trees racing by as he expertly maneuvered through dirt roads and gravel paths that looked barely big enough for his truck. I noted every turn, intent on knowing how to get back to each of my mates' packhouses.

I wasn't terribly surprised to find that Hunter's Shadow Keeper packhouse looked nothing like the Ghost Dancer packhouse. Rather than a hulking mansion with outbuildings, there was one oversized log cabin in a central location with dozens of smaller cabins and tiny homes dotted the open landscape. It was just as breathtaking as Blade's packlands, but in a very different way.

I was growing more excited to meet the different pack members, curious about the people who lived here and eager to learn how they differed from their light counterparts. I wondered how different Glenn's pack was, if they were as night and day as Hunter and Blade's packs, or a little more in the middle of the two extremes.

"Welcome to Shadow Keeper, little mate. I hope you enjoy your time with us," Hunter purred as he opened my door.

"It's beautiful, Hunter. I don't know what I was expecting, but I think this is beyond anything I could have imagined."

He glowed with pleasure at my words, taking my hand and leading me into the main house, where there were probably about twenty people milling about, preparing for the evening.

Unlike Blade, Hunter took me to the side to introduce his parents in a more private setting.

"These are my parents. My mom, Andrea, and my dad, Jerome."

I shook his mom's hand, pleasantly surprised at her excitement, before greeting his father with a quirked brow that Hunter didn't miss.

He narrowed his eyes at his dad, glancing between us. His dad squirmed a bit before reluctantly admitting to our previous interaction, and apologizing for being short with me. Andrea and I were chuckling in the corner like a couple of schoolgirls when Hunter told his dad off for meddling. We ended up leaving them to their bickering, Andrea insisting on showing me around the packhouse.

Overall, Shadow Keeper was much more laid back than Ghost Dancer. I wasn't challenged, either outright or subtly—everyone just seemed happy to meet Hunter's mate and the new Watcher, promising to keep business out of the day and stop by the shop when I was there.

I learned that many members of Shadow Keeper worked with their hands, whereas Ghost Dancer pack members tended to drift more towards white collar work. Andrea admitted that Moon Walker had more of an even spread, with people from all walks of life. They were a more open pack, she told me, with many members that bucked social and cultural norms.

I learned more from the Shadow Keeper members than I did from Ghost Dancer, which I found surprising. I guess a part of me expected that the pack filled with teachers and stockbrokers would be more interested in teaching than the one filled with lumberjacks and plumbers. I was wrong, as assumptions tended to be. Nothing about Wolf Lake and the Shadow Moon territories had been what I'd expected, and it seemed that wasn't going to change now.

I didn't have to fight or prove my dominance at all, I was just promised that I would run by Hunter's side, being his mate.

The main meeting started around six p.m. with a barbecue. Everyone was happy and dancing, and whereas I didn't see anyone under the age of probably sixteen at the Ghost Dancer pack meeting, children were running about here at the Shadow Keeper meeting. When I asked Andrea about it, she explained that Ghost Dancer kept the children below shifting age away from the shifter business so that they could grow up in a more human setting, gradually introducing them as they hit puberty, but Shadow Keeper and Moon Walker took a different approach.

"You'll have to ask Glenn more about Moon Walker traditions, but here at Shadow Keeper, the younglings are exposed to their heritage from birth. Most of Ghost Dancer is sent to human schools before transitioning to shifter schools as they reach puberty, which is when most pups shift for the first time, but we have a dedicated school for any shifters who want their children to grow up in the culture. Some Moon Walker pups attend, as well as a few unaffiliated pups and other types of shifters not associated with our regional packs."

I was surprised by how much I didn't know, and pleased that Andrea was willing to fill in the gaps for me without judgement or puzzles. It was a nice change.

Hunter and his father dealt with various pack issues, took votes on proposals, and welcomed newly shifted teens into the fold once everyone had eaten. It was fascinating watching how expertly the two men ran everything, while Andrea scurried about shaking hands and checking on families. Everyone seemed to have their place, their own distinct role, but with no judgement or persecution if they were struggling.

"Normally, you'd take the role of Luna, if you weren't the Watcher, dear," she told me just before Hunter took the stage to announce preparations for the pack hunt. "As Luna, you'd be in charge of making sure that everyone has what they need to thrive, checking in with families to ensure that everything is good at home, and at work, and with the children and the pack, and arranging celebrations. The Luna accepts people into the pack, having the final say when shifters petition to become new members."

"Oh, wow. How is it going to work then? Is the Luna always the alpha's mate?"

She shook her head and shot me a blinding smile.

"Not at all. Being the alpha's mate is not a requirement. It's just how it usually plays out. Often times, when the alpha's mate already holds a position in another pack, or isn't a shifter, or things like that, then the alpha will choose a trusted shifter to take the position of Luna. It's usually one of the daughters from the Beta's line, but not always."

"Has Hunter chosen a Luna yet, then? Since he knew we were mates and all that..."

"No, dear. He said he wanted you to approve of his chosen Luna, so he's been putting it off."

"Oh."

The fact that Hunter wanted my approval left me feeling warm and fuzzy in a way I didn't expect.

Just then, Hunter took the stage once more, clapping his powerful hands to draw the attention of the crowd. It was time to run.

Children were ushered inside the packhouse, where several women, including those who were pregnant and couldn't shift, had setup a little area for the kids to play and have fun while the mature wolves ran. Andrea had told me earlier in the evening that the people who stayed behind changed from week to week, so that everyone who was able got a chance to run.

Once he had shifted, Hunter trotted up to me and headbutted me until I took my place by his side near the front of the pack.

The feeling of the power of the pack washing over me was just as intense as when I ran with Blade last night, but this time it was warmer, closer to family than anything. We ran as one cohesive group, breaking off into smaller groups to hunt once the moon was high in the sky.

It was exhilarating, freeing, and satisfying. I never wanted to stop, but when we finally did, the residual high from the joined power of so many like-minded wolves was intoxicating. By the time we made it home, it was after three a.m., and I was pleased to have Hunter collapse into my bed with me, both of us succumbing to exhaustion within minutes.

CHAPTER THIRTEEN

My phone vibrating on the nightstand was what finally woke me. I grabbed the thing, intending to throw it, but sense stayed my hand at the last moment, and I checked the message instead. It was from Orin. He'd sent the address, saying that we had reservations at a place in Denver at one p.m. I glanced at the time and groaned. It was already eleven, so I needed to get up and get ready.

The other side of the bed was cold, so Hunter must've been up for a while. I frowned, wondering why he didn't wake me.

I didn't have to wonder long, as there was a note sitting on my dresser.

'Little Mate, I got a call for an emergency repair that can't wait. Wolf Lake Reno & Repair is on the job. You looked so peaceful that I didn't want to bother you.

-Hunter'

The sentiment was sweet, but of course now I had to run to town to grab my car rather than catching a ride. I groaned and dressed quickly, throwing on some ripped jeans and a t-shirt that optimistically said 'I'm the greatest,' before grabbing my keys and stuffing them in my purse and racing out the door. I shifted and tore through the trees, arriving at the trees beyond the shop about fifteen minutes later, panting as I shifted and jogged to my car.

Camille popped her head out of the shop and quirked a brow as I turned the key in the ignition.

"Sorry, Cam, I'm meeting a friend from Oregon in Denver later and I almost forgot! She's going to be so mad."

Camille snickered and waved, slinking back into the shop.

Once I was out of town, I released a sigh of relief. I'd been worried that she'd ask more questions, but she seemed happy enough with my excuse.

Thankfully, the address that Orin sent me was on the edge of Denver closest to Wolf Lake, meaning I was there in plenty of time.

When I pulled into the parking lot of a seedy-looking dive bar, I was confused at first. This was hardly the sort of place I could picture the fae—or any person who valued not being stabbed for looking in the wrong direction. But after sitting in my car for a few minutes, I decided to take the plunge and head inside.

When I walked through the door, it was like everything changed. Instead of a seedy bar, it was an upscale restaurant and bar with private booths that had curtains and doors as well as some open seating.

"You must be Everly," a small woman with ethereal wings greeted me as I glanced around in awe.

I had to blink a few times before I could respond, trying to hold in my shock at her appearance.

This is the world you live in now, Everly. Be cool. Be cool. Be cool.

"Yes, that's me," I replied peppily, cringing a little as my voice cracked.

She smiled and ushered me towards a booth in the back corner, where she held open the curtain to reveal a spacious but seemingly empty booth. I stepped inside, shocked to find that, the moment both my feet were within the confines of the curtain, Orin appeared across from me with a wide grin.

"I almost expected you to stand me up," he said cheerily while I floundered at his sudden appearance.

He rolled his eyes when I didn't say anything, leaning forward to whisper sarcastically.

"It's *magic.*"

I rolled my eyes and crossed my arms, trying to be discreet about rubbing the goosebumps that had appeared along my arms.

"Well? You said you had information."

He chuckled and tossed me a plastic menu.

"Eat first, then we'll talk."

"I'm not hungry," I muttered, blushing when my stomach growled, giving me away.

He didn't comment, but picked up his own menu and chose a summer salad, with strawberries and a raspberry vinaigrette.

I chose a Route 66 mushroom and swiss burger and water, my rebellious stomach growling ferociously while we waited for our food.

I watched him from the corner of my eye as I ate. He was graceful, moving with a sort of sophistication I would expect to find in a regal court. He reminded me of the image I'd always have a royalty, moving with a sort of grace that didn't have any wasted movements.

Once we had both finished eating, he leaned back, waiting patiently for our plates to be cleared before crossing his arms and inspecting me closely.

I sipped on the milkshake I had ordered, trying to keep an unaffected and uninterested look on my face.

After a few moments of watching me, he grinned and leaned forward, resting his elbows on the table and leaning his head on his hands.

"So you're the new Watcher of Wolf Lake. Not quite what I was expecting."

I quirked an eyebrow, making him laugh.

"No, not what I was expecting at all, but not a disappointment. You're positively brimming with power. You may just be able to do what your grandmother couldn't."

He was speaking in riddles. I didn't want to give him the pleasure of seeing me squirm, so I just kept gradually sipping on my shake, watching him.

He laughed again, shaking his head, and glancing casually around.

He was afraid, I could tell. But of what?

"What do you know about the Oberon, young Watcher?" he finally asked, ending our little stalemate.

I slowly pulled back from my shake, setting it on the table before casually wiping my lips and leaning back with a shrug.

"The same as everyone else, I suppose," I said airily.

He frowned, apparently expecting me to go on. When I didn't, he released a gusty sigh and shook his head.

"I know you don't trust me, Watcher. You're right not to, I am fae, after all, and the historical associations between our peoples have no always been…harmonious. This time, however, I want to help you."

"Why would you want to help me? What's in it for you?"

He grimaced and shook his head again, leaning back once more.

"Freedom. Freedom is what's in it for me."

"From what?"

"From oppression."

I rolled my eyes.

"Yeah, that's generally what people want freedom from. Care to be a little more specific?"

He smirked and shrugged, so I picked up my shake again and resumed sipping, pleasantly surprised by the seemingly unending ice cream.

By the time I was sucking on the dregs of the shake, making that irritating slurping noise that accompanies a nearly empty glass, he was growling with frustration.

"The Oberon, as you call it, is just as much of a nuisance to my people as it is to yours!"

"Oh?" I swirled the straw, trying to scrap the creamy goodness from the walls of the cup.

He slammed his hands down on the table between us, snatching the cup from my hands and snarling as he shoved it into the hands of the girl standing beyond the curtain.

"This is serious, Watcher!"

I quirked a brow once more. Now that he was angry, I might get something useful out of him.

He blew out a breath and visibly forced himself to calm down, closing his eyes for a moment while he gathered his thoughts. When he opened them again, they were blazing, a glowing, verdant green that swirled with power. Whoever Orin was, he was a very powerful fae who had been hiding much of himself before. He didn't want us to be seen together, either. He needed me, I knew, which is probably why I was being so bold.

"Watcher. Everly," he said, his voice and eyes softening at my name. "Please, you need to listen to me."

"I'm listening," I said, leaning forward. "There's a whole lot that you're not saying though, Orin."

He closed his eyes and pinched the bridge of his nose, as if begging for patience.

"I realize that I might not be making much sense, and that I'm not giving you much, but trust me when I say that you need to listen to what I am saying. You need to hear my words."

I waved for him to continue before crossing my arms and leaning back, watching him carefully. His manners had changed, shifting from his careful control to an almost desperate, jerking motion. He was serious about needing me to hear him, but something was holding him back from saying what he really wanted to say. I decided that I needed to change tactics. Instead of antagonizing him, I needed to charm him.

"Alright," I said, leaning closer, plastering a softer look on my face. "Tell me what you think I need."

He smiled softly, nodding at me.

"You need to understand that what you call the Oberon has been around longer than you know."

He paused, swirling his glass of wine.

"It used to be called the Darkness, long ago. It's grown, and changed. When it was the Darkness, it was just a disease. It infected people, changing their behavior."

He shook his head, a look of disgust on his face. I waited patiently for him to continue. Whatever he had to say, it was important, I could feel it. And this might be our best—our only—chance at finally learning more about the Oberon.

"When it infected people before, it was obvious. They would have a darkness in their eyes, a musky mask to their scent. Their actions and attitudes would change. They would be obvious when they sought energy to feed on, and they wouldn't recall who they were."

He took a sip of his wine, staring into the glass like a man haunted by the past.

"When they fed, though, they'd get stronger. Faster. Their magic would be amplified, and they'd be compelled to feed more and infect others."

"It's not like that anymore, is it?"

"No," he ground out, running a frustrated hand through his hair. "No, it's not. Now it's more insidious. It infects silently, almost undetectable even to those who have fought it for centuries. It chooses its victims carefully, funneling their power through the shadows. It hunts, and it feeds, and it seeks more."

"What changed?" I ask when he paused long enough to make me think he was done speaking.

He growled and shook his head, swallowing repeatedly like there was something stuck in his throat.

"I can't say," he finally ground out, his voice ragged.

I narrowed my eyes at him, staring into his eyes, which blazed with fury and agony.

"You've been placed under a geas," I murmured quietly.

He ground his teeth and nodded.

I was thankful for all of the information that Blade had been pounding into my brain. If it wasn't for his insistence on me learning everything I could, I wouldn't have recognized the signs of someone fighting a geas—a prohibiting spell of sorts.

"It's related to the Oberon, isn't it?"

His muscles clamped down, his nostrils flaring in fury. Clearly, the geas impacted his motions, too. I couldn't ask direct questions, because nodding his head was out.

"It's alright," I said hastily. "You don't have to talk about the Oberon."

His muscles unclenched and he released a sigh of relief. But I needed that information.

"What was the Darkness?" I asked casually.

His eyes flared with approval. Clearly, the Darkness wasn't part of the geas, but the Oberon was. Curious.

"The Darkness was a disease, of sorts. Magical in nature. It was suspected to have been linked to a—" His mouth clamped shut, indicating that he was too close to the subject of the geas.

The Oberon must be linked to whatever he was about to say. I waved my hand through the air as if dismissing the subject, and his jaw unclenched. He curled his fist, clearly frustrated by his forced limitations.

"So now the energy siphoned is funneled to a source, right?"

He nodded stiffly. We must still be too close to the bounds of the geas. I wracked my brain to try and find a safe way to ask what I needed to know.

"The Darkness has been burned away in the past, though," I stated, watching him carefully.

A small smile appeared on his face as he tipped his head slightly forward.

"I managed to release some of the victims recently. They don't have any memories, at least, not yet. We're hoping they will recover in time, but it seems almost like they were controlled when they had the infection."

He nodded, sipping on his wine.

"Have you been infected?"

"No. I'm too strong for such a thing to occur, there is too much light within me," he said, glaring at me as if willing me to understand.

Light. I had light, and the Oberon wasn't able to infect me, not really. It wouldn't stick. He must have the ability to channel light in a similar manner.

"Not for lack of trying," he grunted while I thought.

I nodded my understanding, grabbing my water and taking a sip.

"So the Darkness could enhance the abilities of those infected, and seemed to funnel that enhanced magic back to a source, right?"

He nodded, the motion once again stiff. The source was the problem with the questioning. There had to be something that controlled the Oberon. Before it would have been a thing, but maybe, now it was a person? The larger shadow, perhaps. It, he, always seemed to be around when I was attacked.

"So the light can burn the shadows away, I've learned. But if someone has been infected too long, it kills them."

He nodded encouragingly as I spoke. I was careful to keep an eye on him, waiting for his muscles to freeze up on him.

"When an infected person feeds, it makes them stronger, but instead of them keeping that strength, it gets funneled to the source of the infection."

I was carefully speaking in generalities, hoping to avoid any specifics that would activate his geas while still getting information that I could use.

Judging from the approving set of his lips, it was working.

"It used to be easy to detect an infected, but something changed, making it harder. I can sometimes smell the difference, though," I said, frowning. "But not always. There are way more of the sha— infected— running around than there are people in the region. It's not possible for me to have avoided running into any infected during my time there."

He nodded encouragingly.

"It would make sense for those close to me to be targets, if the goal is to stop me from stopping the whole thing."

He smiled at me, sipping his wine.

He probably couldn't tell me who was infected, even if he knew.

As I was trying to formulate another observation, my phone began to vibrate. It was four p.m. already. We'd been here for three hours. I had to get going if I was going to make my date with Blade.

I ground my teeth together, not wanting to lose the opportunity to learn more about the Oberon, but Orin's eyes shadowed over and he shook his head.

"Nobody can know that you're meeting with me, Everly. If you miss whatever you have going on tonight, they'll grow suspicious. I'll figure out a way to get you more information, but for now, you need to focus on keeping anyone from knowing of our association."

I frowned. I knew he was right, but this felt too important.

"You will see me again, Everly. Hopefully, sometime soon, you can eliminate the threat and we can both speak freely."

I groaned and smacked my head on the table.

"I don't know enough to stop any of this, Orin. I need more. I'm piecing things together too slowly. It's a puzzle where more than half the pieces have been destroyed, and I'm trying to make my own."

"I know, Everly, and I apologize for that. I'll be at the summit. I'll try to get away before then, hopefully with some way to help you more."

"You've given me a lot to go on, but I know I'm still missing some important pieces."

He smiled softly and nodded, tossing some cash on the table and slipping out from the booth.

I waited a few minutes before heading out, not wanting to risk being seen together since he was so adamant about it being a risk. With his geas, and my inability to consistently sense when someone had been infected by the shadows, I was inclined to agree with his concerns.

CHAPTER FOURTEEN

I made it home just in time to meet Blade for our date. He took me back to the fancy Italian restaurant in the middle of nowhere that he took me on our first date. It was a nice, relaxing evening, and while I was a little disappointed when he didn't try to join me in bed, I was also somewhat relieved to just have a normal evening, for once.

Unfortunately, the normalcy ended the moment my head hit the pillows and my eyes fluttered shut.

*

My eyes opened to a curious scene: Orin, standing before one of the shadowy Oberon, a scowl on his face.

The sibilant sound that haunted my dreams drifted out from the trees surrounding him and the small shadow.

"Such an ungrateful child," the voice hissed while Orin scowled down at the small shadow.

The shadow before him reached up, as if begging for help. He grabbed its hand, holding it in a white knuckled grip.

"Look what I have given you! Look at the power before you!"

"I have no interest in this corrupt power you offer," Orin snarled toward the trees.

The hissing voice of the largest Oberon cackled, leaving chills racing through me.

Orin shuddered and ground his teeth.

"Release Ophelia," he demanded roughly.

"Not unless you take your dear sister's place, princeling."

Orin burst up, fury overtaking his face.

"Is that your price? You will free Ophelia and Lucille, and I will join you," he shouted through gritted teeth.

"Oh, what a delicious trade," the voice said, the largest shadow and another, smaller one stalking into the clearing. "Very well."

The small shadow's movements reminded me of zombies from B movies, stiff and controlled, like the lights were on but nobody was home.

It was terrifying.

The large shadow waves toward the smaller one that accompanied him, making them grind to a jerking halt a few feet from Orin and the shadow he called Ophelia.

"Your sister and your lover for you, what a delightful deal you have struck!"

The shadows parted briefly to reveal the grinning face of the man from my last unsettling dream, the big one who snapped the human's neck.

As I inspected him, I noticed some similarities between him and Orin. The same nose. The same strong jaw. They looked almost like brothers, but no, that didn't feel quite right.

The man, no, the monster, waved his hands towards the two smaller shadows, sucking the darkness from them with the motion before flicking it toward Orin with glee.

The women beneath the shadows both collapsed. The one before Orin was clearly his sister, a younger, more feminine version of him, while the other looked like some fairytale princess.

The monster had said it was a trade for Orin's sister and his lover, so that must be who the other was. Lucille, he'd called her.

I tried to move forward and help the women, a sick feeling in my gut, but my feet were rooted to the ground. I was unable to do anything but watch in horror as the shadows swirled around Orin before forcing their way inside his mouth, eyes, ears, and nostrils.

It was a sickening sight, but Orin's ragged screams made it so much worse. The shadows ravaged him, evacuating him before my eyes.

The monster chuckled, inhaling deeply as Orin screamed, almost like he was feeding off his pain.

When Orin finally stopped thrashing, I breathed a sigh of relief. Too early.

His body contorted backwards as light rushed from everywhere the shadows had touched, viciously purging the darkness from his body.

The monster growled in frustration, sending more and more shadows at him until the light built to a point of exploding out of Orin. The monster stood there a moment, contemplating Orin before grabbing the two women by their hair and stalking away, leaving Orin unconscious and vulnerable in the middle of the clearing.

I was horrified by what I'd just seen, certain that the large Oberon was going to force the two women back into his control while Orin was helpless.

This must be why Orin needed me. I tried to go to him, but I was still frozen in place as the scene swirled and changed.

I was now in an elaborate throne room, watching as Orin kneeled before a woman who looked like she radiated light.

"I have failed, mother," he whispered, his voice catching.

She smiles softly down at him and shook her head.

"No, my love. We just need to find another way. Does the head still stand?"

He nodded stiffly. Her smile turned sad at the confirmation.

"There is still hope, my love. We may be bound to prevent us from acting against him, but there is still another who has not fallen prey to such limitations."

He looked up in shock.

"Seek out Eustice Cummings. She is of the Moon Clan. Her bloodline is the last not wiped out by him. Aid her as much as you can."

He nodded, rushing from the room with a slight limp, his body visibly bruised and battered.

The scene swirled and morphed again, showing Orin kneeling in my living room before grandma.

"Please help us, Watcher."

"I will do my best, Sentinel, but I cannot fix this alone."

"Of course. I will aid you as I am able."

"Good."

The scene swirled and changed, showing grandma in Wolf Lake Manor, staring out the window. Orin was there, on the other side of the glass, a deep frown marring his face.

"They come for me, princeling. There is hope yet. My light is nearly lost, but there is another who can save us all."

He nodded, listening intently as grandma babbled on, most of her words making little sense.

Then she stopped speaking, turned, and seemingly made eye contact with me, a feral smile on her face as she pointed to a framed picture on the wall behind me.

Stiffly, I turned, gasping in shock when I saw the image.

It was me, but I looked so… fierce. I looked like a warrior. My hair was glowing in the moonlight as I fought shadowy creatures, light pooled in my hand. Around me were wolves, dozens of wolves, my mates apparent among them.

"They are the last hope," Grandma's voice rang out with a sudden clarity.

I turned back to face her, finding her face dropping into an enraged snarl.

"They are coming. Be gone, princeling. Find my granddaughter, help her prepare."

"I can't leave you to fight him alone!"

"You can and you will, or your sister and lover will be lost for good. I may yet still be saved, if you find Everly in time. Now go," she demanded, opening the window and climbing out before thrusting her hands forcefully against Orin's chest and marching off.

I blinked back tears as the scene shifted again.

This time, there was nobody around. I was in a dark cave, lined with shackles along the wall.

I shivered as I moved one foot, finally able to step forward.

My body was covered in goosebumps, chilled to the bone as I moved through a seemingly endless network of caves.

The shadows around me seemed alive, but they were not Oberon. No, these shadows screamed silently, agony echoing out from them, the very air filled with unimaginable paid.

'We have been distorted,' they cried out to me without ever uttering a word.

'Save us. Save us. Save us.'

I was confused and overwhelmed, wanting to stop, but my body seemed beyond my control once more, marching inexorably forward.

I was alone here, and in my mind. Somehow, I knew that Treoirn wasn't with me right now, and that knowledge terrified me as my body moved forward of its own accord.

I wanted to scream at myself to stop, but somehow knew that making noise here would be a death sentence.

The further I moved, the colder and darker it grew. I imagined that this is what death felt like, but knew that I wasn't dead. Not yet.

I kept moving, one foot in front of the other until my body ground to a creaking halt in the center of another dark, cavernous space. This one was different.

It was filled with water. All around me the floor was water, and I was somehow walking on, or suspended above it. I spun in a circle, seemingly in control of my limbs once more.

The water was a sickly, glowing blue, with shadows writhing within it. There, directly below me, submerged in the center of the pool, was a glowing, pulsing, shadowy, purple formation. It looked like a cluster of gems, but no gems that I had ever seen. They appeared to be alive, and screaming in agony.

'Help us.'

'Help us.'

'Help us.'

A thousand layered voices echoed out at me.

'Gaelana. Gaelana. Help us. Save us,' they chanted wordlessly, overwhelming me.

"How?" I whispered hesitantly.

'The beast.'

'The king.'

'The monster.'

The voices shouted soundlessly at me, each giving a different response. I shook my head in confusion, until the voices coalesced into one.

'The crystal!' they shouted, making my mind rattle with the force of their echoed words.

'Power. Souls. Drained. Distorted. Unnatural. Save us. Save us. Save us.'

My eyes fluttered closed, the strength from their shouting dragging me into darkness.

When my eyes opened next, Hunter was staring down at me, his concerned gaze anchoring me back in the real world.

"Are you alright, little mate?" he asked softly.

I reached up and stroked his face, nodding. He helped me sit up, watching me with a frown.

"What's wrong, Hunter?" I asked once I was seated on a pile of pillows.

He shook his head, blowing out a worried breath while inspecting me closely.

I stroked his face again, patting the bed beside me. When he didn't move, I huffed.

"I'm fine, Hunter. What's wrong?"

He grumbled and settled in beside me, crossing his arms, his brow furrowed in thought.

"Hunter!" I barked, startling him.

He glanced at me sharply, blowing out another breath.

"You were gone, Everly," he whispered brokenly.

I frowned, confused. "What do you mean? I've been right here all night."

He shook his head and rubbed his chest, inspecting me again.

"No, I mean, you were gone. The bond, it was gone. Almost like you were..." he trailed off, not willing to say the words, but I knew what came next.

He felt the bond leave him, like I was dead. I shuddered as I remembered the cave. It reminded me of the cave of souls from an old myth that I read while in school.

"What do you mean, Hunter?" I asked in a shaky voice.

He drew in a deep breath before pulling me close to his chest.

"You were gone, Everly. Our mate bond didn't snap, it just wasn't there. It was like it didn't exist, like you didn't exist. And then I came in here, and you were asleep, but I couldn't see you breathing. I had to check, I had to make sure you were alive, so I came closer... I couldn't hear your heartbeat, and your chest wasn't moving." He said all this in a monotone, sounding broken.

I was worried about his words, and him. I didn't want to hurt him, but what I'd seen was important, I knew that. I wouldn't have been shown otherwise.

When his breath caught in his throat, I pushed the memories of my dreams, no, my visions, to the side and threw myself into his arms, crashing our lips together.

He kissed me like a man who was drowning, and I was his first breath. He pulled me as close as he could, wrapping himself around me and consuming me with a branding series of kisses before pulling back and burying his face in my hair, heaving with heavy breaths that reminded me of the sobbing voices in that cave. I hugged him to me, worries about those trapped voices, trapped souls, raging through my mind.

We had to stop the Oberon.

The sun was rising, casting an ethereal glow across Hunter's dark hair. He looked angelic, like some prince of darkness come to claim my soul, and I couldn't help but kiss him again before getting out of bed and tugging him along behind me.

"Blade, Glenn," I shouted out my door. "Family meeting downstairs in ten minutes!"

I heard my other two mates scrambling out of bed, enjoying the sight of Hunter's growing smirk as I led him downstairs to the living room where we sat, him in the large recliner, and me in his lap.

I noticed that Glenn had added a picture of Hunter as he worked on building something in the woodshop attached to his packhouse. Glenn had caught the glistening sweat on his brow and the look of concentration on his face as he worked.

Hunter saw me admiring his portrait and chuckled.

"Glenn was working on it this week. He said you wanted one of each of us, and then one of all of us."

I nodded dumbly, awed by Glenn's talent once more—and the

masculine beauty of his subject. Hunter kissed the back of my neck, sending shivers racing down my spine as I admired the painting. If what I had to tell my mates wasn't so important, I'd drag Hunter back upstairs and have my way with him right now.

Glenn and Blade barreling down the stairs, both looking deliciously disheveled, derailed my thoughts and startled a chuckle out of me.

"You two look terrible," I said.

Blade scowled and Glenn laughed.

"I was up all night finishing that," Glenn said, waving at Hunter's portrait.

"It looks wonderful, Glenn, thank you."

He smiled and dipped down to kiss my cheek before plopping down on the couch and sprawling out, much to Blade's disgust as he was forced to take the small loveseat, furthest from where I sat in Hunter's lap.

"If you recall, Everly, we didn't return home until nearly three a.m., and I was up after you went to bed, looking for the answers to some of your questions."

I grimaced at the reminder. I had asked a few questions about the Oberon before we started our date, and Blade had promised to look into things for me.

"Right. Sorry about that. This is important or I wouldn't have woken you guys up."

Blade's eyes softened as he nodded before turning curious. He inspected Hunter, noting the dark circles under his eyes, and his mouth pulling down in a worried frown.

"What's wrong, Hunter?" he demanded, but Hunter just shook his head, like the wound was too raw to pick at.

Too bad we didn't have any choice, because the Oberon was a greater threat than any of us had realized, and there was no more hiding from it.

CHAPTER FIFTEEN

Glenn noticed Hunter's strange behavior and sat up, his shoulders tensing. No longer was my happy, fun-loving mate lounging on the couch, and in his place the warrior, Alpha of the Moon Walker pack, sat ready to battle whatever was threatening us. The sudden change had me shaking my head in awe as I gathered my thoughts.

Orin was very adamant that I couldn't tell anyone who wasn't bonded to me, but sitting here with my mates, I wasn't sure that I could keep this from them. I wasn't sure I should try. I glanced back at Hunter, thoughts racing through my mind. Maybe I could swear them to secrecy or something. How would I even make something like that stick? Perhaps a geas of my own? I didn't even know how to create a geas though. And I'd never want to use such dark magic against anyone I cared for, stripping their souls, their freedom like that…it was beyond reprehensible. The pain I'd seen in Orin… No. I banished the thought almost before it crossed my mind, but not so quickly that I wasn't appalled the thought had existed in the first place. Except…shit. Anyone could have taken that information from Orin, forced him to share what he knew, if it hadn't been locked behind the geas. Giving them this information and then leaving it unprotected could put a target on their backs, and that was the very last thing I'd ever want.

I was so lost in my torment that when Blade cleared his throat to draw my attention back to the conversation at hand, I almost fell off Hunter's lap. If Hunter hadn't been holding me so tightly, I might have.

"Hunter. Silver," Glenn said softly, watching us with a worried frown.

I closed my eyes and blew out a breath, steadying myself.

"I think this conversation might be best had over some tea," I murmured, taking in the weary looks on all of my mates' faces.

Glenn agreed, slipping from the living room to start the kettle while we slowly made our way to the kitchen. Hunter reluctantly pried his arms from around me, allowing me to fall back beside Blade while he helped Glenn.

"What's wrong, Everly?"

"How does one create a geas, Blade?"

His face looked like he'd sucked on a lemon as he contemplated my question.

"There are a few different ways, most are unpleasant. Generally, dark magic is involved if the person being placed under the geas isn't willing."

"And if they are? Willing, I mean."

"Then it can vary, it could be as simple as an agreement sealed in blood. Those are the simplest, and the easiest to break if there's nothing else binding the agreement."

"I see."

"Why do you ask?"

I shook my head, taking my place at the table. Blade decided to sit across from me, where Glenn usually sat. He must want to have a clear view of my face for this conversation, not that I blamed him, with the odd questions I was asking.

Glenn placed a cup of chamomile and honey tea before me, Hunter adding a plate of cookies. I thanked them before looking back to Blade.

"Are there any other ways to make sure things remain a secret? Binding ways that block people from intentionally or accidentally speaking of something?"

Blade frowned and nodded slowly.

"There are blood contracts. The contract would include terms for breaking the contract and would generally include safeguards to prevent the information from spreading."

He inspected me closely, waiting for Glenn and Hunter to take their seats before questioning me further.

"What is all this about, Everly? What's going on? And why was Hunter so shaken?"

I grimaced. "It's complicated, Blade. What it really comes down to is that I have new information about our enemies, but that information spreading beyond the four of us could be life or death."

"So you want to place a geas on us?" Blade seemed a little offended, but not angry, which was…something, I guessed.

I swallowed nervously, inspecting each of my mates and weighing my words.

"I don't want to, no, but…I think it might be necessary. It's not just our lives that would be at risk if I told you all what I've learned in the last twenty-four hours. Some of the secrets I know now aren't mine to tell. My source didn't bind me, but he warned me that anyone not mate-bound to me already could be a risk if they knew this information. He didn't—couldn't—explicitly say it, but I got the feeling that the Oberon might be able to pull information from your mind if you don't have access to the kind of light magic that is within me to block it."

Blade sucked in a sharp breath, unease lurking in his eyes, though whether at the revelation or the thought of the geas, I wasn't sure. Hunter looked grim, and Glenn sad, like they both already had an inclination that such was possible.

"Do you think a geas would prevent us from being vulnerable like that?"

"We could always bond, if that's your concern," Glenn murmured, a displeased frown on his face.

He didn't want our relationship to move on someone else's time, I knew, but he was willing to go faster than we wanted if I asked it of him. The realization made me both happy and sad at the same time. I was thrilled that Glenn would do anything for me, and upset that there was so much pressure on us.

"No, I don't think rushing things is the answer, love," I told him with a soft smile.

He took my hand and kissed my knuckles.

"I'd do whatever you asked of me, Silver," he murmured.

"The geas idea might be a viable option," Hunter said thoughtfully. A steely determination stirred in his eyes.

"I was thinking that, if I wrapped some of my light around the geas, it might shield the knowledge in the same way that the mate bond does," I said softly. "But if you know any other way, or if you tell me you don't want me to do this, then I won't force you."

Blade nodded, stroking his chin.

"It could work. But limiting our ability to share vital information could hurt the cause."

I was already shaking my head before Blade finished.

"No. We can't share this with anyone. We have no way of knowing who's infected. We can't risk it."

Blade frowned, confused by my statement without the knowledge I was withholding. After a few moments of contemplation, during which I sipped on my tea and nibbled my cookies, he nodded.

"Alright, Everly. I trust you. To place a geas on willing hosts, the simplest way that would work for your needs is probably a blood bond. Infuse your light into it."

He went on to explain the nuances of the geas blood bond. It involved multiple steps. First, we needed to mingle our blood, all four of ours, in a bowl. Then I needed to infuse the blood with magic. Each of us needed to sip from the bowl, and then, I would have to slash each of our palms, fusing them together while saying the oath I needed for the geas. It was both simple and complicated all at once. A single misstep and the geas might not take.

I was grateful that Blade was willing to walk me through the process, and that they were willing to submit to such a binding oath. Technically, Hunter didn't need to submit, if Orin was to be believed, but he was willing despite everything. Or perhaps because of it.

The sight of the blood in the wooden ritual bowl that Blade pulled from my grandmother's office made me queasy, but I managed to hold my nausea in, infusing the crimson liquid with light until it glowed, and sipping on it. I passed the bowl to Hunter while trying not to gag. He sipped, then passed it to Glenn, who repeated the process before passing it to Blade.

Blade finished the liquid, setting the bowl on the table between us before pulling out a wicked-looking dagger.

"Technically, you only need to say the oath once, and we could make a circle, but it would be a stronger binding if you did it once for each of us," Blade admitted, still sporting that deep frown of displeasure.

He might be doing this of his own free will, but he didn't like it. Not that I could blame him. I didn't like it any more than he did.

We decided on the more secure solution, with me slashing my hand and repeating the oath three separate times. We came up with a simple, but effective oath.

"Do you agree that what is spoken about here, any secrets unveiled or discoveries that could bring harm to hidden allies, will be spoken of only between those in this room, in safe spaces where the information gained today cannot be overheard by others?"

"I agree with your request," Hunter said, the first to take the oath.

"So it is said, so shall it be," I repeated the words Blade had told me seal such a binding, flinching at the flash of light, the burning sensation between my and Hunter's clasped hands.

We repeated the process with Glenn, and then Blade, the burning sensation worse with each of them. When I asked about it, Blade assured me that it was because Hunter and I had already sealed our mate bond, so the binding didn't need to go as deep to settle in as it did with Glenn and Blade.

"Since we already have a link, it's actually less painful than it would be with someone who you had no magical affiliation with," Blade said with a grimace.

Once the binding was finished with all three of my mates, the residual blood in the bowl on the center of the table flashed before disappearing in a puff of smoke.

"That shows that the binding took," Glenn murmured, rubbing his now-scarred palm.

"Will the scars heal?"

"In a few hours they'll be barely noticeable," Blade promised.

I nodded in relief, finishing my tea and dropping my head into my hands.

"You need to get on with it, Everly. There's only so long that we have to speak words that will be covered by the geas," Blade told me, his voice surprisingly soft.

I groaned and leaned back in my chair, glancing at Hunter before blowing out a long breath and facing Blade.

"So you need to know that I was visited at the shop the other day by a man... he wasn't a shifter. I didn't know what he was at first, but Camille told me he was fae."

I held up my hand to prevent Blade from interrupting when he opened his mouth.

"Please just let me get everything out before you begin with the questions or scolding."

He nodded and clamped his mouth shut with visible effort. I gave him a grateful smile before continuing.

"Camille and the man, Orin, didn't seem to like one another. It wasn't as simple as a shifter not liking a stranger, though. I'm not sure what the problem was, but when he saw Camille, Orin sniffed the air and stiffened before passing me a card and disappearing. He was discreet, and I got the feeling that Camille shouldn't know who he was or that he left me anything, so I hid it and told her that he seemed lost."

I blew out a breath, thinking back to that day while sipping my tea.

"He called me Gaelana," I said simply, frowning.

Blade opened his mouth to speak but shook his head and snapped it shut again, waiting for me to continue.

"I called him later that day, and we arranged to meet down in Denver. He was adamant that nobody who wasn't already bound to me could know. Hence the geas," I told them, meeting each of their gazes.

Glenn nodded encouragingly, giving me the strength to keep speaking.

"At first, I thought it might be a trap, but he sounded so desperate. And my instincts said I needed to know what he had to say. Grandma always said to trust my instincts."

I frowned, studying my nails for a moment while trying to put the feeling into words. I couldn't, so I moved on.

"I met with him, and he told me some things that didn't make sense. It was like he was speaking in circles, until I asked a question directly about the Oberon. His jaw froze up, he kept swallowing like there was something stuck in his throat. When I asked him to nod to a direct question, his muscles froze too."

"A geas," Glenn said on a breath, his tone both awed and disgusted.

"Yeah. I get the feeling that he wasn't a willing participant. Once I realized that he was under a geas, I started asking more vague questions that would help us with the information we needed. I was able to discover that the Oberon is older than we thought, but before, it was just called The Darkness. When it was called The Darkness, it was a disease that could be scented and seen. It was visible in the host's eyes. The host would be driven to feed, but wouldn't know who they were. When they fed, their power would be stronger. Orin was able to tell me that the shadows could be burned from a host, and they could be saved if they hadn't been under for too long."

Blade was nodding like he already knew everything I was saying.

"Apparently, that strength no longer remains with the host when they feed," I told them, making eye contact with each, willing them to understand what I was trying to say. "He couldn't outright say, but I get the feeling that the siphoned energy gets funneled to someone who is controlling the diseased and the shadows themselves."

Blade stroked his chin and nodded while Glenn looked furious. Hunter was still and silent, like a mask had settled over his face that blocked all of his emotions. I was worried about him, but needed to get all the information out, so I squeezed his hand and continued speaking.

"At that point in time I had to leave. Orin was insistent that we can't be seen together, but promised to be at the council meeting. He's a Sentinel."

Blade frowned, looking like he was flipping through a mental catalogue to place Orin's name and status.

"Hunter, you're probably wondering what all of this has to do with tonight."

He nodded stiffly.

"Well, when I went to sleep, I saw memories... visions, I guess, since they weren't my or Treoirn's memories. I saw that man who was arguing with the humans in my dream from the other day. Well, no, I guess I need to start before that. I saw the big shadow, the one that keeps attacking me, who seems to be controlling the others. And I saw Orin. He was holding a smaller shadow in his arms. He was yelling, telling the man, that monster, to release his sister, Ophelia. The big shadow came out and made a deal, saying he'd release her if Orin submitted himself to the shadows. Orin said he needed to release both Ophelia and Lucille, who the shadow revealed was Orin's lover. Orin agreed, and the shadow dragged another smaller one into the clearing. He ripped the shadows from the smaller two, and opened a gap in the shadows surrounding him. That's how I know it's the man who killed that trapper. He sent the Shadows at Orin, but they didn't take. Light exploded from Orin. When we were talking he admitted that he has power similar to mine, but because of the geas, he can't act directly against the Oberon."

Blade was gritting his teeth, fury shining in his eyes.

"The scene changed to Orin kneeling before a throne, telling a woman who he called mother that he had failed. She said there was still hope, and told him to find my grandma. The scene changed again, and showed him talking to grandma while she was at Wolf Lake Manor. I think I saw what happened right before she ran out to try and fight the Oberon, when I saw her dragged away."

CHAPTER SIXTEEN

I shuddered, remembering the cave.

"After that, I was pulled somewhere else, but it wasn't a memory. It wasn't the past, I think it was now. And it was dark, and cold. I couldn't control myself, my feet just kept moving forward, and I got colder and colder, until I stopped in this big cave. It was filled with water, but the water wasn't... I don't think it was really water," I said with another shudder. "I looked down and could see faces in the water, and at the very center, there was this dark crystallized formation. It was pulsing with power. I was so cold."

Hunter pulled me into his lap. I was shivering, almost like I was back in that cave.

"There were voices, and they asked for my help. They said I needed to stop someone, but there were so many voices and they were all yelling at me. They called it 'The Beast,' 'The King,' and 'The Monster.'"

I was shivering so hard that my teeth were chattering, like I was connected to that place again. The next words that came from my lips weren't in my voice, they weren't in my control.

"The Crystal. Destroy the Crystal. The source. Power. Souls. Drained. Distorted. Unnatural. Save us. Save us. Save us."

I clawed at my throat with trembling hands as the preternatural power filled me, suffusing me with terror. It was one thing to lose control of myself when I was dreaming, but another, more terrifying experience, to not have control while I was awake.

The power left me just as quickly as it had come, leaving me falling forward in Hunter's arms, gasping for breath.

By the time I was able to look up into his eyes, they were blazing with a mixture of rage and fear. He kissed my forehead before piercing Glenn and Blade with a sharp look.

"I woke because I couldn't feel her. I couldn't feel our bond. It was like she was gone. It never snapped, it just ceased to be. I went to check on her and she wasn't breathing, her heart wasn't beating," he told them steadily, a thread of rage underlying his words.

Blade's face pinched as he inspected me. I pulled myself together, squared my shoulders, and faced him once more.

"That was the end of my dream, that cave with the... souls. I think I've heard of something like that before, Blade."

He nodded, his frown deepening.

"It sounds like the Cavern of Souls from Greek mythology," he said softly, glancing at Glenn, who was stroking my hair while Hunter rubbed my back.

We sat in silence for several minutes, each lost in our own thoughts. A flash of light from the bowl, which was still sitting between us, made me gasp.

"The geas is set," Blade murmured. "Everything you've told us will remain between us so long as we live."

I nodded, releasing a breath I hadn't realized I was holding.

"You said that the disease could be burned from them... and we have evidence of that from the last battle. But those who survived have no memories of their time under the influence of the Oberon," Hunter said, his voice rumbling against my back.

"I know. I'm hoping that, in time, they might remember," I replied, scooting back into my own chair, smiling a little when Hunter released an irritated growl.

"With this information, I have other avenues of research that I can focus on. Right now, let's put our attention toward gathering allies for the council meeting. You need to focus on that, and training. Eventually, we'll have to face this 'Beast,' and hopefully put an end to the Oberon, once and for all. But you need to be ready, and right now, you're not. Focus on learning more about your magic, Everly, and we'll look more into the background of the information you've brought us."

I wanted to argue, but I was too tired. Blade must've seen it in my eyes, however, because he smirked and shook his head.

"Don't worry, I'll make sure to keep you updated on anything I find, Mate."

I smiled gratefully at him before wrenching myself out of my chair and traipsing upstairs.

"I'll be down for training in twenty minutes, guys," I shouted down the stairs.

I was sure Hunter would give me the day off, but Blade was right: I wasn't ready to face this threat, and I needed to be, sooner rather than later.

With Glenn's hints from the other day, I was able to finally eliminate the other dummies and move onto the rest of Hunter's training regime. It was miserable, but I had a new determination in me. Before, the Oberon was an abstract threat. Yes, I had been attacked, but I knew I could take care of myself. Now, I knew that there was something worse going on than just some shadow monsters trying to lure me into the open.

After we finished training, I called Camille and told her I would be pretty busy for the next couple of weeks, preparing for the council meeting. She assured me that the shop would be fine, and agreed when I asked her to direct any Watcher requests towards the Lodge.

Both Hunter and Glenn had plans for the day, but Blade was more than happy to set up shop at the Lodge and go over a few things about the packs.

"So I have the run with Moon Walker tonight, but I wanted to make plans for a few meetings here, like a meet and greet, to get to know pack members better," I told him while pacing back and forth along the open floor plan of my new meeting place.

"Well, we can invite the packs a few people at a time... We could go by rank, or age, or anything you want." He checked his smart watch and nodded. "We have four weeks that we can use to prepare and have these meetings before the summit."

I nodded, pacing back towards the oversized kitchen.

"What about the summit, what's the plan with that?"

"As of right now, I have a few close friends feeling out the council members to see who would side with us. We're also going to be training with a few members from the packs starting tomorrow, so they'll be able to submit testimony indicating you're working hard to prepare properly for your Watcher duties."

"Good, that's good. Should I run with all three packs each week?"

"No, I think you should go on tonight's run with Moon Walker, meet them, learn a bit about their pack, and then focus on meeting everyone here. Pick one pack each week to run with, make it a tradition, like the third week is Moon Walker, the first Shadow Keeper, or whatever schedule works best for you."

"That makes sense... Why don't we stick to the order we're already in: Second week Ghost Dancer, Third week Shadow Keeper, and Fourth week Moon Walker. Then we can use the other time for meetings here."

"That would work. It will also allow you to build a kinship with all three packs."

I whirled to face Blade, narrowing my eyes at him.

"What?" he asked.

"Well, I was running with Shadow Keeper, and Andrea told me about the Luna position and how it works for them... how does it work for Ghost Dancer? Your parents weren't very... informative."

He grimaced and shook his head.

"The Luna is the mate of the alpha."

"But I'm not tied to the pack, and I'm your mate."

He frowned and nodded.

"We'll have to find another way to make it work."

"What about the mate of your Beta? Or do you have any sisters, or cousins?"

He tilted his head to the side, as if considering my words.

"I do have a female cousin, and she's already pretty tied in with the Luna duties. I'll have to ask the pack elders what they think."

"Would it be a risk? Would her mate want the alpha position?"

He chuckled and shook his head.

"Her mate is the most timid man I've ever met. There's no way he'd be even remotely interested in being alpha."

"Oh, that's good. Can I meet them?"

"Yeah, I'll be sure to introduce you at one of the meetings. Speaking of, how do you want to do them?"

"What do you mean?"

"I mean, we can have all pack meetings, with everyone of the same age group or rank or whatever, or single pack meetings."

I thought about that, an idea sparking at his words.

"The packs don't get along, do they?"

"Not usually."

"Maybe we can change that," I said thoughtfully.

Blade laughed, pulling me in for a hug.

"If anyone can, it's you. Besides, since you're a neutral who is mated to all three alpha apparents, you have a bit of an edge."

"I do, don't I?"

He bent down, kissing me deeply. I melted in his arms, enjoying the feel of not having to worry about anything. Blade took control, angling me just how we both needed, and ravaging me with kisses.

I never wanted him to stop, but as always, he was in complete control of himself, pulling back with a wicked smirk while I was panting with desire.

He picked me up effortlessly, and placed me on one of the new bar stools Glenn and I had ordered not too long ago before stepping back and crossing his arms. I could see the bulge in his pants, but he acted like it wasn't there, or like it didn't affect him at all. One of these days, I would make Blade lost control for real.

But apparently, not today.

"We'll have to give up date nights for my plans to work," I said simply.

"I had figured as much. Next week. Have your dates with Glenn and Hunter this week, and next week we will start the meetings. This week is for getting to know the packs a little."

"Right, we'll do a deep dive next week. It also gives us time to arrange things, put out notices and all that."

He nodded in agreement, sitting beside me and pulling out a tablet to begin our plans. We ultimately decided on breaking the first set of meetings into age groups and doing mixer-like events. We decided to have three different separations each week, the first being age, the second rank, and the third was to be open to anyone who was interested in coming. Blade checked on the preparations Glenn and I had made, commending me for the foresight of ordering dozens of sets of collapsible furniture and extra serving ware. By the time we finished checking on everything, arranging the notices, and planning the menus and schedules for the meetings, the sun was touching the tips of the trees.

"Silver, it's time to go," Glenn shouted from outside, making me grin.

Glenn promised to pick me up at six, and it was five to now. He was punctual. I liked that. I kissed Blade's cheek before scurrying out of the

Lodge, leaving him to finish the final touches and reach out to the individual Elder Alphas with our proposition.

"Hey there, gorgeous. Busy day?"

I filled Glenn in on the plans Blade and I had made while we hiked towards his packhouse, which he had sheepishly informed me was less than a ten-minute hike on two legs from the lodge.

"Since our pack is a bit smaller than the other two, we don't need as much space for the living areas," he confided to me as we broke through the trees.

I was awed by the Moon Walker packhouse. It wasn't as rugged as Shadow Keeper, nor as frilly as Ghost Dancer. Moon Walker's packhouse looked almost like my own house, just bigger. There was a wraparound porch, several porch swings, two stories and an attic. The house itself was probably double or triple the size of my own, but it still managed to look cozy. There were probably two dozen other, smaller houses. They looked like what you'd expect to find on a ranch or farm, and I was utterly charmed by everything.

"Welcome to the Moon Walker pack," Glenn whispered in my ear, making me shiver.

He smiled down at me, grabbed my hand, and tugged me forward, taking off at a trot that I found easy to keep up with. By the time we reached the main house, I was breathless with delight.

Once he opened the door to the main house, we were ambushed by three women. Well, they were more like girls, the eldest being maybe sixteen.

"Calm down, ladies, there is enough Everly to go around, just wait your turn!" Glenn shouted as the smallest girl scaled his back, cackling with glee.

I was laughing along with their mirth when a tall man and kindly woman joined us in the front room, soft smiles on their faces. The woman looked like a female Glenn, which made me smile. The smallest girl definitely took after their father, while the other two looked like a cross between their parents.

"Annie, down, now!" barked the man once he had calmed down from his laughing fit.

"Aw, but Papa, Glenn never comes home anymore!"

Her mother smiled and pulled her off Glenn's back, setting her on the floor. She zoomed around the room with her arms out, making airplane noises, much to my amusement. Glenn laughed and shook his head, pulling each of his family members in for a hug before stepping back and pulling me forward.

"Ma, Pa, ladies, this is Everly, my mate and the new Watcher."

His mother smiled softly at me and grasped my hand in hers, patting it maternally. I was overwhelmed by the soft touch, and for a moment even a little envious. Glenn deserved to have a caring family. She saw the watery glint to my eyes and pulled me in for a hug, whispering in my ear.

"It's okay, darling, Eustice told me about your mother. You're home now, and you can consider me your surrogate mom. We'll make sure you never have to wonder if you're loved again."

Glenn's dad ushered his kids towards the oversized living room, which looked like it could easily seat forty people.

"Now, how about some tea?" Glenn's mom suggested. "And then we can meet everyone properly."

I nodded and followed her to the kitchen to help with the tea. While we worked she chatted away, telling me about how their pack was run. I found that most of what Andrea had told me about Ghost Walker was accurate, and Amira—Glenn's mom—was happy to correct any misconceptions without making me feel bad.

Back in the living room, we placed the tea, cookies, and small sandwiches on the coffee table and sat down next to our mates.

"Now, dear, this is my mate, and Glenn's father. His name is Gerard. Our eldest daughter, she's fifteen, is Sandy. Then there's Jasmine, but she goes by JJ, who is twelve, and you already met Annie, sort of. She's five."

I greeted each person in turn, filled with awe at their easy interactions. So this was what a proper family felt like.

We chatted for close to an hour before Gerard hefted himself up with a groan and marched outside.

"It's time for the run, dear," Amira said happily, clapping her hands and ushering Annie and JJ upstairs.

"Some weeks we have a full meeting and barbecue, but that's usually only once a month. Today is just a run and hunt. Dad still deals with most of the pack issues while easing me into the alpha role."

I was shocked, since it had seemed like Hunter and Blade were handling most of the pack responsibilities for their packs, then again, Glenn was the youngest of the three, so I guess it sort of made sense.

Amira told me that she was staying behind with the younger two tonight, because she wanted to get to sleep early, but usually the children were all watched by the local coven on run nights. She said they had moon parties while those who could shift ran. It was odd to me, but after Glenn explained things, I could see how that would work better for them.

Once again, the run was exhilarating, filling me with energy and power. The thrill was different this time. Instead of feeling like I was being fueled by shadow or light, I just felt free. Like the chains that had been tying me to one thing or the other had snapped, and I could just bask in the purity of being me. The freedom of running as a wolf, frolicking and channeling the power of the in between, no longer split between one or the other.

We ran until the moon was high in the sky, and at midnight, I felt the shiver of power that raced through the pack, imbuing me with more strength than I thought possible. I'd have expected the dark or the light to be stronger, especially with their higher numbers, but I could tell, without a doubt, that the Moon Walker pack had more potent magic.

Wasn't that just the strangest thing?

CHAPTER SEVENTEEN

The weeks flew by, the time until the council summit ticking away like the sands in an hourglass, always moving even when I wanted and needed them to slow.

The first set of meetings we arranged to be a teen and young-adult-only meeting, figuring there'd be less deep-seated prejudices and age-old grudges to handle that way. We had everyone from age fifteen to twenty from all three packs lounging around the Lodge. Blade, Glenn, and Hunter set up various stations with games, activities, and training exercises so the rowdy young shifters could show off and relax all in one secure location. We had food lined up along the kitchen counter and drinks spread out. At Blade's recommendation, Glenn and I removed all the alcohol from the Lodge, which I had to admit was a smart suggestion. We ended up with about sixty or so people at this meeting.

Their fathers were reluctant to consent to a gathering without anyone older than their sons, but once we explained our goals of uniting the packs against the Oberon, they gave their agreement, encouraging everyone to attend each meeting they were qualified for without making it a requirement. It turned out to be a good strategy, as only two or three pack members within the age range were absent. We only had to break up one fight, directing them to the training area to settle their dispute. Afterwards, the two young men were hanging out like long-lost best friends. I bonded with many of the teens, learning about their hobbies and hopes and dreams, and filling my phone with dozens of new contacts.

The next meeting was for adults and their children, with anyone under fifteen and adults from twenty to forty-five. It was the bulk of the packs, but went surprisingly well. Of the nearly one hundred and fifty people who showed up, only two or three butted heads, and it was more of an angry soccer mom thing than any pack animosity.

The men from the various packs bonded over beers and barbecue while the women and kids raced around, some playing and some relaxing on the beach chairs we had set out. It seemed we were making great progress with bringing the packs together, and I was eager to keep things moving towards unity.

The third age-divided meeting was for the pack elders, and anyone who didn't have kids under fifteen but was forty-five plus themselves. A few people who came to the adult and family meeting also joined us here, having been over forty-five but with children below shifting age. I was worried at first about how people would feel about the divisions we had set, but it turned out that everyone enjoyed it, the few people who attended the family meeting coming up and thanking me for throwing these parties, as we had dubbed them to encourage participation.

When all was said and done, only ten individuals from all three packs skipped all the gatherings, and three of them were from the same family who was out of town visiting colleges.

We treated the first set of meetings like parties, playing games, and having fun with food and drinks. The goal was just to meet everyone in a relaxed environment and make contacts, which worked like a charm. My phone was bursting with new contacts and texts from the various pack members, much to my mates' delight.

The next set of meetings we held were based upon rank, and were more formal. We started with the lowest-ranked members from all packs and worked our way up until we had the Alpha, Beta, and Gamma families from all three packs seated at a long table, breaking bread and discussing news. By the end of that meeting, we had gotten everyone on the same page: the Oberon was the enemy, not each other, and we needed to work together to stop it. It had gone better than I'd dared to hope, but then, there was no pack that hadn't been affected by the Oberon, and it was the one thing they all hated more than each other.

The final meeting we planned was just one large gathering with everyone from all three packs being invited. I had attended one more run with each pack, and was much more comfortable with the majority of the residents of Wolf Lake. We planned the last meeting as an end-of-summer bash the Saturday before the council summit.

The last meeting was a sort of test of how far our progress had come with the packs. Everyone came, even those who had been out of town or opted out of the first couple of meetings. The place was so crowded with bodies by noon, that I was concerned we might not have gotten enough food. Andrea, Amira, and Calisto, Blade's mother, came to my rescue, however, swooping in to direct the staff we had hired to help with the event and even helping cook and arrange things themselves at one point.

A few fights broke out among the rowdier pack members, but nothing serious. All in all, everyone had a great time and went home full and happy, content with the new alliance of the packs. Once everyone was gone for the day, leaving just me, my mates, and their parents, I finally breathed a sigh of relief. It felt like all our preparations were paying off.

"You know, when you came to me with this idea, I thought you were crazy, son," Blade's father, Drake, admitted, sipping on a glass of wine.

Blade shrugged and grabbed a beer, sinking down on one of the couches. I took the spot next to him, while Hunter and Glenn settled in around me, Glenn happily sliding down to the floor and leaning his head back on my lap while I ran my fingers through his hair.

Hunter and Glenn's parents each grabbed drinks before choosing their own seating place while Blade's mom joined his dad, leaning against him and looking relaxed for the first time since I'd known her.

"You all did well with this plan of yours," Jerome agreed, sipping on a wine cooler.

"The packs are more at ease with one another and united than they've been since I was a child," Gerard murmured, kissing Amira's hair and thanking her as she passed him a beer.

"Are you kids prepared for the Summit?" Andrea asked with a worried frown.

Calisto glanced at Andrea, having a silent conversation with the other Luna.

"I know you've been training with members from all three packs," Calisto began, passing Drake her diet coke and leaning forward earnestly, "but have you gotten their statements yet? You need to show a pattern of progress. Everly has handled five disputes since starting her duties as Watcher, and has publicly agreed to ramp up her duties to a full load mid-September, but without establishing the pattern, I'm worried you won't be able to convince enough people on the council."

Blade and Hunter shared a look while Glenn leaned back, staring up at the ceiling.

"We have the statements," I assured their parents. "They were submitted on Friday, and I've made copies just in case they get 'misplaced.'"

"Good, good. And do you have enough support with the council?" Andrea asked, a worried frown on her face.

I'd really grown to care for all three sets of parents, enjoying their company and being welcomed into their families. It took Blade's parents a couple of visits to drop the mask of indifference, but now that they had, I felt like I could confide in them.

"We have identified at least twenty-five members of the council who are definitely compromised," Blade confirmed with a frown. "They called a full summit, which makes me think there are more than that. Likely, those they have influence over are spread throughout the world, and they're hoping to fabricate enough evidence to sway those who are traditionally neutral."

"If they're not certain enough in their position to require a full summit to deal with the issue, then you have a chance to sway the council with logical arguments," Drake said thoughtfully.

Jerome nodded, finishing his drink and setting it aside.

"I've submitted a character witness report for Everly, and made copies for you. I was also worried about parts of your defense being 'misplaced,'" he said, growling the word.

"Likewise. I've also compiled statements from individual members from each pack, as well as those involved in the mediation incidents. We also have a statement from Miranda and her daughter in regard to the attack in June. As you know, I recorded your training session this morning, and Hunter recorded your first training session, so we'll submit those into evidence as well to show your progress," Gerard said, pulling his wife closer when she growled.

Andrea was furious with this whole thing, having had the council try to frame her husband for some bullshit charge once before when they were younger.

"It'll be okay, Mom," Hunter said.

"You need to expose these fuckers, Hunter. I'm tired of my family being targeted for doing what's right!"

We all nodded our agreement, slipping into silence. It was Glenn who broke the heavy stillness, hopping up and stretching before turning serious eyes to face me.

"We've done all we can to prepare, Silver," he said seriously.

I nodded, exhaustion pulling at my limbs.

"The Summit is in five days, at the Boulder Council House, which is one of five the Council Houses in North America."

Blade had explained to me that each continent had ten Ley Bound counties, or Ley Spots. Each of those spots had a Watcher, Sentinel, Keeper, and Guardian who were responsible for maintaining The Balance within their county. Each of those positions granted you a place on the Balance Council, which oversaw the greater happenings in the world, monitoring The Balance. Each was a hereditary position. Normally, Blade had said, a council meeting had just three elected officials from each continent's Balance Champions, as we were known. Since this meeting was called as a Summit, however, every Champion will be present. Summits were generally only called once every other year, but this was the second this year, the first being around the time Grandma fell ill. She wasn't able to attend it, of course.

I had learned a lot during the last few weeks, and my brain was positively bursting with the information. Apparently, during this meeting, Grandma's place as Champion-Elect for the Greater Balance council would be filled, in addition to me being on trial for whatever bullshit this Giovanni dude was spewing.

Beyond the Balance Council, there was also a Council of Elders who were elected to govern supernaturals. They were elders, always over the age of sixty, I learned, who were elected from each supernatural archetype. Three from each continent for each archetypical race. Grandma had been on that council as well, so that position also needed to be filled at this meeting. Unlike the Greater Balance Council, the Elder Council members didn't have to be Champions, which was why I was confused as to why the Balance Council elected them. Blade confirmed, however, that it was actually the general populace that elected them, and the full Balance Council just confirmed the vote, similar to how the Vice President and senate in the USA confirm the vote during presidential elections.

I was lost in my spiraling thoughts, trying to recall every bit of information that might help me survive past next week, when Glenn's soft words drew me back to the present moment.

"We've done all we can to prepare, so now we need to rest. There's no point in pushing so hard that our bodies are too tired to react when they need to."

I reluctantly agreed with his assessment, letting him pull me to my feet. Blade and Hunter followed Glenn's lead, ushering me upstairs to the oversized bed and bedroom that Hunter had included in the lodge for me in case of late meetings.

"We'll resume our training when we get back from the meeting," Hunter assured me.

"Thank you for coming, everyone. I really appreciate all the trouble you've gone to in order to help me," I called over the railing.

"It was our pleasure, dear," Amira said, pulling her husband up and out the door.

"If you need anything at all, don't hesitate to call," Calisto told me, frowning as she stalked out the door, Drake on her heels.

Andrea chuckled and tugged Gerard up, swatting his ass as he marched out the door. She winked at me over her shoulder before glaring at her son.

"You take care of Everly, Hunter. I don't want to have to go down to Boulder and deal with those assholes myself."

He grinned and shook his head, blowing his mother a kiss before pulling me back toward the room.

"We'll head down to Boulder on Tuesday so we can meet with a few allies and make sure there aren't any traps set," he told me, grabbing a change of clothes and herding me towards the bathroom.

"Take a nice bath and relax," Glenn said, lighting several candles along the edge of the oversized soaking tub.

I swear, Hunter made sure that my bed, bathtub, and shower were big enough to house all four of us, even if we were in our wolf forms.

"We'll finish cleaning up while you take some time to decompress," Blade said, kissing my forehead and retreating back downstairs.

I felt positively blessed to have such caring mates. I wanted to show them how much I appreciated them, but their coaxing was too tempting. I let Hunter and Glenn set everything out, prepare my bath, and arrange the pillows on the bed just how I liked them, giving in to their demands that I relax without wasting any breath protesting. They were right, I needed to decompress, and as much as I wanted to jump their bones and solidify the bond between all of us, now wasn't the time. I refused to be pushed into tying them to me out of fear. It would happen eventually, and from a place of love and deep satisfaction, not fear for the future.

I slid down into the hot water, melting into the steam and losing myself, just for a little while.

CHAPTER EIGHTEEN

Tuesday came too soon, and before I was ready, we were piling into Glenn's souped-up Escalade. I hadn't seen it before, so asked where it came from when he ushered me into the passenger seat.

"This is the vehicle I use for all official Council stuff... it's top of the line, all the bells and whistles... and bulletproof." He murmured the last part under his breath and I arched a brow.

"Bulletproof, seriously? Do you think we're going to be shot at?"

The look in his eyes was anything but reassuring, so I shut my mouth and climbed inside, letting the guys handle my bags—because they'd seemed to take it as a personal affront when I'd tried to do it myself. They were ready for anything, which was even more apparent as they tossed probably a dozen bags of various weapons in the trunk alongside our actual clothes and electronics.

When Blade and Hunter climbed into the back seat, it was with grim looks of determination. We really were going off to war, it seemed.

We drove in relative silence, each of us buzzing with energy. I was both excited and apprehensive about the coming meeting. We hadn't learned much more about the Oberon since we were so busy focusing on uniting the packs and preparing for the Summit, so I was somewhat worried about how we were going to deal with the threat the shadowy creatures posed, but I shook the worries from my mind. I couldn't afford to split my attention when there was such an obvious threat already staring us down.

We made it to Boulder without incident, Glenn driving by the council house to give me an idea of where we'd be going before retreating to check into our hotel. Thankfully, between Glenn and Blade, we didn't need to worry about funds. I wasn't doing so badly myself, having earned more than a few dollars for the five or so disputes I had mediated in the last month, but Glenn and Blade were far beyond me in their earnings. Glenn had just sold another painting for nearly two million dollars and Blade's family owned several companies and stock brokerages that left them flush with cash. I wasn't sure about Hunter's financial situation, and didn't want to pry. We all took care of our own things, but Glenn and Blade ensured that everything about this trip was handled by them.

When we pulled up to our hotel, Glenn drove straight to the valet, not a care in the world as he passed his keys over to the pimply-faced teen and led me to the front desk to check-in.

"Reservation for Glenn Thorne. I booked the penthouse for several nights."

The woman at the desk shot Glenn a blinding smile, ignoring me as she clacked away on her keyboard.

"Ah, here you are, Mr. Thorne. It says you requested three nights with the option to extend, is that correct?"

"It sure is. We might be here as long as a week," he said, tucking me into his side.

The woman curled her lip when she saw the motion, switching her voice from the saccharine fly trap to a more businesslike tone, much to Hunter's amusement. I glared at him when he chuckled, narrowing my eyes when he grabbed Blade and disappeared into the little lobby bar.

"Alright, sir, you're all checked in. Here are your keys, it says you requested four, is that correct?"

"Sure is. Thanks."

She tucked the keys into an envelope, scribbled a number and name on it, and passed it to me, now ignoring Glenn, much to my amusement.

"The number for your personal concierge is on there, he'll handle any request you have from dry cleaning to tickets to a show. I'll be at the desk until six p.m. Breakfast can be ordered to your room or taken downstairs between seven a.m. and nine a.m. Room service is available from five a.m. to midnight."

"Thanks," I said, grabbing the envelope.

The envelope had instructions on how to access the penthouse suite and information about checkout time and how to extend. I passed it to Glenn before heading to the bar to grab Hunter and Blade.

We spent the rest of the evening in the room, going over potential scenarios with the council and discussing the known and unknown entities we'd be dealing with.

The day of the Summit arrived faster than I would have liked, and before I realized it, I was dressing in a smart pantsuit and heeled boots. Hunter, Glenn, and Blade were each wearing a suit of their own, their ties matching the green of my shirt perfectly.

Despite Blade's hours of preparation, going over every little nuance of how the Summit would work, I was still taken by surprise when each of my mates was led toward their designated seat while I was ushered to a slightly raised platform in the center of the coliseum like room. I felt like I was being led to the executioner.

The platform that I was led to had two tables, reminding me of a modern courtroom. In front of the platform was a raised dais-like space with three seats, one higher than the other two. Blade had told me that there would be a presiding elder who oversaw the trial, and two representatives, one from the defense and one from the prosecution, to counsel the presiding elder. All three seats were empty, so I wasn't sure who was going to oversee this whole thing.

Once the room had filled up, an elderly-looking shifter took his place in the presiding chair, banging a gavel on the desk before him.

"Order, I call this Summit to order!" he shouted in a gravelly voice.

The room grew silent immediately. Whoever he was, he had everyone's respect.

"Now, our first order of business is the trials. Who brings charges?"

A man behind me cleared his throat and stepped down, moving to the opposite side of the platform I was ushered to.

"I do, Elder."

"State your name and the charges you bring."

"My name is Giovanni Aricci, Watcher for the Sicilian Ley Spot, and I bring charges forth against one Everly Anderson, Watcher for the Wolf Lake Ley Spot." Giovanni paused and glanced around, seemingly trying to make eye contact with as many people as possible.

The Elder rolled his eyes and growled.

"Stop playing games and state your charges, Aricci, or drop them."

Giovanni dipped his head, a contrite look plastered on his face that set my teeth on edge.

"Of course, Elder. My apologies. As we all know, attacks by the Oberon have been increasing lately. I have it on good authority that the bulk of attacks have tripled within the bounds of Wolf Lake since Everly has taken over as Watcher. She has failed in her duties. I recommend that she be removed and exiled, bound so that she can no longer bring harm to those around her."

The room burst into a cacophony of voices. The elder banged his gavel furiously, demanding orders. Once the room was silent once more, he glared down at Giovanni and spoke.

"Who here supports your claim against Everly Anderson, Watcher of Wolf Lake?"

Giovanni twirled around, calling a name I had never heard. I gasped when I saw the face of one of the people who was infected by the Oberon, one of the people who was freed when my light burned the shadows from them. Their eyes were cold, and filled with hatred when they looked at me.

"I support the claim. I am Tristan Eir, and I have witnessed Everly

Anderson's failure as Watcher first-hand."

The elder banged his gavel again, glowering at Giovanni.

"Everly, do you have anyone you'd like to request join you in your defense?"

I nodded, calling for my mates, who came rushing down the moment the elder permitted. Giovanni snorted, turning his back on us and pacing towards the end of the platform.

I was pleased to find Glenn's dad taking his place beside the elder as counsel for me, but when the counsel for Giovanni took their place, and the room began murmuring once more, it was impossible not to feel worried.

The elder had Giovanni and Tristan present their case, leaving me reeling at what was said. Apparently, Tristan and his family were all infected by the Oberon at the same time. He claimed that it was when I arrived in Wolf Lake, and that my failure to cleanse the shadows in a timely manner cost his wife and children their lives. His argument was compelling, making even me question if I was doing enough. When the elder leaned over to hear his advisors speak, my stomach churned with worry.

"Thank you for your testimony, Tristan. Giovanni, do you have any other evidence to present?"

He didn't. The elder waved for me to stand and present my counterargument.

"Thank you, Elder. We have submitted in advance testimonies from many members of Wolf Lake's packs."

A frown creased his wrinkled face further, and he turned to quickly speak to a man standing beside him, who shook his head.

"There has been nothing submitted by the defense," the Elder announced—not surprising me in the least. We'd expected Giovanni and his ilk to try some stunt like this, and I was glad I'd been forewarned, because even now my stomach was tying itself in knots.

Glenn's dad ground his teeth together and whispered into the elder's ear, leaving him nodding in agreement.

"If you have copies of these testimonies with you, you may submit them now."

We did. It took the Elder nearly an hour to read through everything and present the evidence to the council, leaving the room murmuring once more.

Hunter, Blade, and Glenn each took a turn speaking, talking about how I knew nothing about the supernatural before coming to Wolf Lake, and how, within just a few months, I had gone from a human with no combat experience to a warrior and Watcher who was uniting the packs of Wolf Lake behind a common cause. The council seemed split, arguing amongst themselves by the time we had finished presenting everything.

"Giovanni, do you have anything you'd wish to say before a vote is cast?"

He did, of course.

"As you have all seen, Everly Anderson is directly at fault for at least three known deaths, probably more that have yet to come to light, due to her inaction. Her inability to act as Watcher has devastated families, and cannot be tolerated. Allowing Miss Anderson to sully our sacred duty is an affront to all supernatural kind, and a hazard to Wolf Lake."

I was reeling by the number of people nodding in agreement. Had they not listened to anything we had just said? How can I be held at fault for something that was going on before I was even aware of this world?

"What exactly are you asking for, Giovanni?" asked a voice from the crowd.

"I'm not asking for anything, merely making suggestions."

"Then what are you suggesting?" the voice asked acerbically.

"What I'm suggesting, is that we find someone more... competent.

Clearly, this child can't handle the responsibilities of being a Watcher," he sneered.

"So you're suggesting that we remove the last of the Moon Clan from her role, because, why? She's young? You were young once, too—though granted it was a long time ago." A few titters met this remark, but he pressed on. "Should we have replaced you when your father died, leaving you to be your regional Watcher at the ripe old age of fifteen? Who do you propose to replace her, a robot?"

"Of course not, but I had a lifetime of preparation. This girl doesn't even know about the boundaries or why things are as they are."

"Perhaps that's for the best," chimed in another voice. "Maybe, because she doesn't know everything that the others do, she can act without the limitations that we've placed upon ourselves. Young people can grow and learn, but people who already know everything are stuck in their ways."

Giovanni ground his teeth, glaring in the direction of the second voice.

"We cannot allow such incompetence to stand!" he said through gritted teeth.

"All I see is a girl who was thrust into a new world and is now working tirelessly to find her place and help people," said yet another voice.

The crowd murmured in agreement.

"A girl who has three mates! She's monopolizing three of the strongest alphas in the country!" Giovanni shouted, trying to regain some of his traction.

"He makes a good point," someone agreed.

"Nobody needs three mates, and she's already bound one of the alphas to her." I could hear the sneer in that voice, and it left me feeling small.

"So spare the girl. She has already chosen her mate, leave it at that."

Shouts of agreement rang out, leaving me reeling. Did they want to take my mates from me? What the hell? They couldn't do that, surely!

The Elder banged his gavel again, demanding order.

"We will put it to a vote!" he shouted. "All in favor of binding Everly Anderson and electing a new Watcher line for Wolf Lake, raise your hands."

About thirty hands around the room shot into the air, leaving Giovanni grinding his teeth in frustration.

"Noted. Everly Anderson will retain her position as Watcher of Wolf Lake and take up her seat on the Council."

At jeering from the crowd, the elder called another vote, sounding tired.

"Very well, very well. All in favor of declaring Everly Anderson and Hunter Rowan as mates, and severing the bond between Everly, Glenn, and Blade, raise your hands."

This vote took longer, the elder having to count and recount until he stared around in disbelief.

"It's a tie," he declared, frowning. "Everly Anderson, I'm afraid that you will be unable to seal your mate bond with Glenn Thorne and Blade Aspen until a meeting with the Elder Council can be called to settle the matter." He frowned and glanced around. "Please take your seats, Wolf Lake Champions. Let us move this meeting along to other matters."

Blade and Glenn were fuming as we marched to our seats. I'd have thought that Hunter would be happy, but the scowl on his face told me otherwise.

We watched as the elder bent down to speak with Glenn's father, nodding in agreement with something before sending Gerard off and calling the rest of the Summit's agenda to order.

We spent the rest of the day voting on various measures, confirming recent elections, and dealing with all manner of bullshit that I had no interest in.

By the time everyone was released, the sun had long since set, and exhaustion was etched so deeply into everyone's faces that I thought it would take a month of sleep to erase it.

Thankfully, because of the long day, we didn't have to attend another meeting tomorrow, which meant we could head home rather than hang around here.

When we made it back to the hotel, Glenn's father was waiting for us in the lobby. We took him upstairs and ordered room service, settling in to discuss the idiocy from the day.

"I'll work on the council," Gerard said over dinner. "They won't block a Goddess-Blessed mate circle."

His support, though welcome, wasn't enough to take the sting from my fury.

"The Councils have no right to put their noses in our personal business. Who I mate with is up to me, not them!"

"We'll figure this out, Silver," Glenn reassured me, touching one hand to my arm lightly…and nothing more.

I didn't see how we could possibly fix this, but I didn't want to refute Glenn, so I just gave in when he led me to bed and tucked me in, falling into a restless sleep filled with Giovanni's laughing face and shadows looming over me.

CHAPTER NINETEEN

Once we were back home, I found myself angry. Angry at the council. Angry at Giovanni. Angry at the jealous voice that tried to convince others to take my mates away from me. I took it out on my training partners, railing against the world mentally while pummeling wolves three times my size.

We worked every day, ramping up my training in preparation for facing the Oberon. I barely touched any of my mates, despite the roiling urge to say fuck this and have my way with them. The lack of contact and the lack of progress toward eliminating the Oberon threat made me even angrier, filling me with an all-consuming rage that had me lashing out.

It was not until Glenn pulled me away from Hunter that I realized I needed a break.

"Sorry, guys," I muttered, stalking inside and ignoring the look my mates shared.

I didn't know what day it was. I was going through the motions of life, letting my mates direct me from event, to run, to mediation. I was good enough at hiding my fury from the packs, but when it was just the four of us training, like this morning, I lost control. I could feel it slipping through my fingers and it was hard to care. I felt guilty about potentially hurting Hunter, of course I did, but I wasn't ready to face him, or my reeling emotions, so I drowned my rage in the shower, letting the water wash away my emotions until I was numb.

I was just stepping out of the shower when Glenn appeared in my room, a soft smile on his face, and I felt guilty all over again. He was the one who was being denied a mate—at least I already had Hunter, but he would have no one if the council had their way. I didn't know how he could remain so calm in the face of such terrible news.

"You alright, Silver?" he asked, pulling me to him gently.

This was the first time one of my mates had held me since the summit. Not for their lack of trying, though. I just didn't want to be touched. I was always pulling away when they tried to comfort me, so consumed by anger at those people for trying to keep us apart.

I realized, with horror, that *I* was keeping us apart. Instead of pulling from my mates, I should have been basking in their presence, enjoying what time we had since our happy little life could be ripped from us in a moment. I went limp in Glenn's arms, heaving sobs overtaking me at the memories of how cold I had been.

"Shhh, shh, it's okay now, Silver, it's okay. I've got you, love," Glenn whispered soothingly, rubbing circles along my back as I curled up in his arms.

By the time I had cried myself dry, the house was still and empty, Glenn and I the only people around.

"Do you feel better?" he asked softly.

I nodded, wiping my nose and sniffling.

"Thanks," I mumbled. "Guess I needed that."

"You need to relax, that's what you need, Silver."

I started to protest, but clamped my mouth shut when I realized he was right. I *did* need to relax. I needed to get away from the responsibilities and the negativity that the council had awoken in me. I needed bright and happy and... Glenn. I needed Glenn.

He saw my protests die and tugged me up and into his arms. I giggled between sniffles as he carried me downstairs, bridal style. I felt so small in Glenn's arms. Like a delicate flower rather than the person, the warrior, who was tasked with eliminating a centuries-old threat.

"Now that I've finally got your attention," Glenn teased, making me blush with shame.

I had been ignoring them, neglecting them. I wouldn't blame any of my mates if they now wanted to take the council up on their offer of breaking our tether.

"It's time to go have some fun." He arched a brow in challenge. "No more grumpy Everly, got it? She's banished for today."

I stuck my tongue out, then whipped my head round as I realized he was carrying me outside. I tried to get him to put me down, but Glenn just tightened his grip and dashed into the forest, me in his arms. He ran through the trees faster than I'd ever seen him move, making the canopy above me blur. It was an intoxicating feeling, rushing through the trees in Glenn's arms, feeling his strength wrap around me. I felt free, and loved. Protected.

Tears were torn from my eyes, the wind whisking them away before they could leave a trail on my face. I tilted my head back, just enjoying the ride, relaxing fully in Glenn's arms.

When we stopped moving, Glenn smiled down at me.

"Much better," he murmured, kissing my cheek and flipping me upright so I could slide down his body.

I shivered at the feel of him, letting my hands explore his chest as he slowly set me down. His eyes were filled with heat when I glanced up, a true smile on my face for the first time since the summit.

"There's my mate," he whispered, capturing my lips with a panty-melting kiss.

I was soaked with need, desire to solidify our bond pulsing through me, when Glenn pulled back, growling. I tried to climb him, to wrap myself around him, but he smirked and shook his head, pulling away.

I groaned and stomped along behind him, grumbling to myself about stubborn mates and idiotic councilmen.

When he stopped, I almost ran into him because I was too worked up with cursing the aching need between my thighs, much to his amusement as he stepped aside and grabbed my shoulders, slowly turning me to face a vast lake in front of us.

My breath escaped me in a rush at the sight. It was probably the biggest lake I'd seen since coming to Shadow Moon. The light from the day reflected on its gleaming surface, the trees and mountains and flowers mirrored in the still water. It was beautiful. It was breathtaking and awe-inducing.

"Welcome to Wolf Lake," Glenn rumbled in my ear, making me shiver.

"This is Wolf Lake?"

He nodded against my head, trapping me beneath his chin and pulling me back against his chest.

"This is where the Goddess blessed the first shifters. The Shadow Keeper pack began here, Ghost Wolf merging with her first human."

He speaks the truth, Treoirn murmured in my mind, speaking to me for the first time since my not-so-little meltdown began.

"It's amazing."

Glenn chuckled against my back, just holding me, allowing me to bask in his presence.

I turned in his arms, inspecting him closely before releasing another heavy sigh, the last of my anger melting out of me.

"I'm sorry, Glenn. I've been a terrible mate lately."

He silenced me with another scalding kiss, pulling back just as I was trying to climb him again. He chuckled when I growled in irritation.

"You have nothing to apologize, Silver. The fact that you were so angry about the council trying to keep us apart actually tells us that we mean more to you than you've admitted out loud."

I frowned at his words, realizing that he was right. I never really admitted to my mates just how much I wanted them. How much I needed them. I opened my mouth to tell Glenn as much, but he placed a finger on my lips and shook his head.

"We know, Silver, we know. We need you too. Now," he turned me to face a little clearing further down the shore. "Let's have lunch."

He led me to an elaborate picnic setup, with pillows and blankets lining a recessed sand pit.

"Did you do all this by yourself?" I asked in awe, admiring the ten foot by ten foot hole in the ground lined with blankets and pillows.

Glenn grinned and helped me step into the recessed space. It was at least half a foot deep.

"Nah, Hunter and Blade helped. We figured you could use some time to destress."

I frowned, wondering where my other two mates were. Glenn saw my face and laughed, kissing my hand before helping me to sit.

"Hunter's pack meeting is tonight, and Blade is chasing a lead about your Cavern of Souls."

I shivered at the mention of that gaping cave.

"So it's just you and me today, sorry to disappoint," he said with a cheeky grin.

I chuckled and shook my head, kissing Glenn's cheek.

"You could never a disappoint, Glenn," I told him, leaning back on the pile of pillows behind me.

He beamed, and began pulling food out of the fancy picnic basket in the center of our little space. He placed container after container of food around me, opening them to reveal all my favorite foods, leaving me laughing with delight.

He fed me, not allowing me to do anything besides point imperiously at my next desired morsel. It was relaxing and fun as I lost myself in his good humor and doting ways.

When we had finished the food, he quickly packed the containers away, refusing my help again, before pulling one last container out with exaggerated grace.

I quirked an eyebrow at his happy grin, my face dipping into a frown as he lifted the lid to reveal an elaborate slice of chocolate cake.

"Happy birthday to you!" he sang teasingly, making me frown in confusion.

It wasn't my birthday, was it? It couldn't be. The council meeting was on September 1st, and my birthday was September 23rd. Monday... Hunter's pack ran on Mondays. I could feel a look of horror cross my face at the realization. It was Monday, September 23rd. It was my birthday, and I was so lost in my pointless anger that I had almost missed it. I had lost nearly four weeks to the rage that had filled me.

The thought left me sad and deflated. Four weeks wasted.

"Happy birthday, to you," Glenn finished with a flourish, swiftly lighting the single candle in the center of my cake and steadying it in front of me.

I clenched my eyes shut, begged the universe to let me keep my mates, and blew out the candle.

Glenn handed me a fork and the container before clapping happily, a wide grin on his face.

"You should have some," I told him, offering him a bite.

The heat in his eyes as he slowly leaned forward and slid his tongue up the fork, pulling the piece of cake into his mouth and slowly chewing, savoring it, had my mouth dry with need. When he leaned back and licked his lips, I followed the motion, tempted to set the cake aside indulge in a different kind of dessert.

Stupid council.

Glenn chuckled, his eyes roving over me as I finished the cake, miraculously resisting the urge to jump him.

He was slinking closer, stalking me, his movements filling me with anticipation, when the trees began to shake. We both paused, glancing around uneasily.

Sometime during our teasing, the sun had set, leaving us shrouded in darkness. Clouds blotted out the moon, casting an ominous glow from behind their heavy, gray surfaces. I slowly sat up, inching closer to Glenn as we tensed, waiting for something to happen.

We didn't have to wait long, as moments later, the sky opened up, raining fat droplets of icy water down, just as the trees around us erupted with shadows. They were everywhere, slithering from the smallest cracks, jumping from the tallest trees. Some of the shadows weren't even bipedal. The sight gave me pause.

Were they shifters infected with the darkness, the Oberon, or was it evolving again, now able to drain the magic and life from simple forest creatures as well as people? I didn't know, and I wasn't sure that I wanted to find out. Unfortunately, it didn't look like we were going to have a choice.

Glenn and I slowly rose to our feet, carefully moving from our little den, trying to reach even ground as the shadows closed in and the rain raged. I expected to hear that sinister voice, the grating, sibilant laugh that belonged to the monster, the beast that controlled the shadows, but it never came. Instead, there was a raspy voice. One I didn't recognize, but that sent just as many chills racing through me.

"Watcher," it hissed. "You cannot save us. You have forsaken us," it wheezed, sounding almost like it was sobbing.

"No, I haven't given up," I swore, not sure if I was talking to the shadows, or the person with them.

"He wants you to," the voice moaned, its raspy hiss leaving me shivering. "Go," it choked out, with obvious pain.

I glanced at Glenn, nodding in agreement as he bolted through the trees, back toward home. We were nearly halfway there when the shadows streamed around us once more, descending upon us. Glenn lashed out, directing the rain to create a vortex, which dragged some of the shadows from our path. I reached for my light, intent on burning the shadows from the people and trying to saving them, but one of them latched onto my wrist and began sucking, pulling my essence into them. My light.

It shouldn't have been possible, but they were drawing my light out of me while Glenn watched in horror. I tried to pull away, but the shadow's grasp was too strong. I was so distracted trying to free myself that I didn't notice Glenn's absence until I heard him shout. He was moving further away, and I was growing weaker.

I turned back to the shadow clinging to me and growled, sending a burst of light through them that had them pulling back and screeching.

I took off after Glenn, some part of my mind grateful that he was being dragged closer to home rather than further away.

I had a ball of light readied by the time I caught up to him, the effort nearly dropping me to my knees. He was being dragged by two large shadows. I stumbled after them, lobbing the light at the larger of the two. It didn't burn the shadows away, but it was enough to make the creature to drop Glenn and turn towards me with a hiss. The second shadow limped along, trying to drag a thrashing Glenn behind them, when the sound of howls pierced the air.

The shadows seemed to share a look before turning and hissing at me. The one dropped Glenn, who thunked roughly onto the forest floor, before racing off, back the way we came.

I bolted forward, unsteady and aching. I dropped to my knees beside Glenn, roving my hands over his body. I couldn't find any injuries, but I could smell the musky scent of decay that I associated with the Oberon on him.

"Not again," I moaned, leaning down and pressing myself against Glenn with a sob.

He shook me gently, wiping my tears. We were both soaked from the torrential rain. It took us a while, but we finally managed to slip, slide, and stumble our way back to the house, collapsing on the porch stairs.

Blade came rushing out at the sound of our heavy bodies falling against the wood, a deep frown on his face. He took one look at us before jogging back inside and getting some towels.

We stripped on the porch, shedding our soaked clothes and marching inside, two shivering messes.

"You were attacked," Blade said, that deep frown pulling at his eyes.

"Yeah," Glenn panted out, opening his towel to reveal a bloody gash that I hadn't seen before.

It was weeping black, sending bile racing to my throat.

"You need to bond," Blade said simply, running his hand through his hair.

Glenn gnashed his teeth together and looked away.

"I don't care what the council says," Blade continued, pacing back and forth. "They can't fault you for bonding to save his life, and once you're bonded, they'd have to kill the alpha of one of the strongest packs in the country to undo it. They won't risk it."

I grimaced, unable to fault his logic, but the pain in his voice gave me pause, and I searched his face. And that was where I saw it. Blade thought he'd be cut from our circle once Glenn and I bonded, the council retaliating against us for not waiting for approval.

I stomped up to him and yanked his face down, demanding his surrender with my mouth. He melted against me, taking my comfort and offering his own. When I finally pulled back from our bruising kiss, he nodded, a small smile on his lips.

"You're mine, Blade Aspen. You, and Hunter, and Glenn. You're all mine. The council can try to take you, but I won't allow it."

He grinned and squeezed my ass, planting another possessive kiss on my lips before pulling back.

"There's my feisty mate. Go save our Seer. You and I will have our day," he told me, disappearing out the door and leaving me alone with Glenn.

CHAPTER TWENTY

I tried to rush Glenn, ushering him upstairs and demanding he bond with me before the shadows could do more harm, but he was a stubborn man, refusing to rush through things.

"No, Silver," he said softly, stroking my face. "Just because we're being forced to do this earlier than we had planned, doesn't mean we're not going to do it right."

His words were so similar to Hunter's when we were forced to bond to save his life, that I couldn't help but chuckle softly. My mates were so much alike, and yet so different, all at the same time.

Glenn tugged my hand into his, kissing the back of my knuckles before pulling me closer and sweeping me off my feet once more. He stumbled a bit before righting himself and marching upstairs, his mouth a thin, determined line despite the obvious strain.

"Glenn, I can walk," I told him softly.

He ignored me, continuing to carry me up the stairs despite the strain. His breath was coming in gasps when we finally reached my room, but still, he stubbornly held me in his arms, carrying me to the shower and gently setting me down. I shivered at the heat in his eyes, the determined look that told me this night was just getting started.

Happy birthday to me, I thought, inspecting his defined abs.

I reached forward, intent on tugging the towel from his waist, but he grinned and stepped back, capturing my hands in his and shaking his finger at me like he was scolding me. I scowled, but the look just made him chuckle and dance away.

He backed towards the tub, turning the water to its hottest setting and closing the plug with a grin. There was no way I was getting in that if it was as hot as it looked, but I was certain that Glenn had a plan, so I just plopped down on the closed toilet and watched him work.

He carefully measured out some Epson salts, added a dash of the rosemary, lavender, and rose bath herb mixture, and lit all the candles along the edges of the tub. Once he turned off the obviously scalding water, he grinned back at me and scattered fresh rose petals on top. I had no clue where he'd gotten them, which made me suspicious.

He saw the look on my face and chuckled.

"It *is* your birthday, Silver. I had planned to pamper you no matter what," he said simply.

I nodded, pretending that it was obvious, and nervously crossed and uncrossed my legs while he disappeared into my bedroom. I wanted to follow him, but the bone-deep weariness that filled me from whatever that shadow did had me too exhausted to move a muscle, which seemed to suit Glenn just fine, so I wasn't too worried.

I must've dozed off, because the next thing I knew, Glenn was shaking me awake, a mischievous smile on his face and steam swirling through the bathroom. The shower was running, and he was standing before me in all his naked glory. I was half convinced that this was some dream that my addled mind concocted, the stress of everything having finally cracked me.

Any thoughts of me dreaming fled the moment his fever skin touched me, though. He was very real, and very ready, and very mine.

I purred as he lifted me into his arms, effortlessly carrying me into the shower. Either he had recovered some of his strength since the attack, or he was too excited to notice his own fatigue. Either way, I was eager to feel his skin against mine.

He carried me into the shower and gently placed me on the large, built-in seat before grabbing the showerhead and rinsing us both off. When I tried to grab my loofa and wash myself, he tsked me and hung it out of my reach. I pouted, until he squirted a dollop of shampoo into his hand and began massaging my scalp.

I was putty in his hand, leaning against his delectable flesh and resisting the urge to lick my way down his washboard abs. His erection was impressive and hypnotic, waving back and forth in front of me while he kneaded my scalp. Every time my eyes fluttered closed, I'd force them back open to admire his impressive length, imagining taking it in my hand and working him the way I did in my dreams.

Every time I gathered the strength to reach up, however, he'd scrape his nails along my scalp, sending shivers of pleasure racing through me and forcing my traitorous eyes to close and relax while I moaned in pleasure. I never wanted his hands to stop working me, and yet I desperately wished for him to stop distracting me and let me mount him, the way my body so desperately craved.

Once he finished with my hair, he helped me to stand and began washing every inch of me, leaving my whole body rigid with desire. I kept begging him to touch me where I really needed him, but Glenn just chuckled and kissed my nose, continuing his ministrations. I was a mewling mess by the time he finished. He gently guided me back towards the bench, helping me sit, before quickly washing himself. I watched him eagerly, hoping for a bit of a show, but he just quickly soaped up and washed off, grinning smarmily at me.

Once we were both squeaky clean, Glenn insisted on scooping me back into his arms and carrying me out of the shower. I protested when he moved my dripping body to the bed, but he ignored me, making me laugh when he haughtily presented me the bed, which was covered in fluffy towels and lined with candles. Once I stopped protesting, he gently placed me on the center of the pile of fluffy towels, and grabbed another from beside the bed, quickly drying himself while I watched.

This time, he gave me a bit more of a show, but it was still over too soon.

I smirked and gave him a saucy wink before trying to sit up and drag him into the bed. Once again, he danced out of my reach, chuckling at my pout.

"It's your birthday, Silver. You can't do any work. Let me pamper you."

I grumbled, crossing my arms and leaning back. He rolled his eyes and stalked forward, wagging his finger at me when I tried to reach out once more. I finally gave up and flopped back on the bed, squealing when he grabbed my feet and dragged me down towards him. Once I was in his arms, he captured my lips in a sweet kiss before flipping me over and producing another towel from out of thin air.

I was breathless and needy, but Glenn was insistent on doing things his way, so I relaxed against the pile of towels and let him slowly dry me off. He worked my body, clearing every drop of water before tossing the towel aside and grabbing another one, which he wrapped around my hair and began to massage my scalp once more, the towel muting the sensations enough to allow me some semblance of focus.

I couldn't tell how long he worked my hair, but by the time he finished, my locks were mostly dry, and somewhat tangled. He piled pillows up and had me lay on them with my head on my arms, and began gently brushing my hair.

It was the most sensual thing I'd ever experienced. I didn't know that having someone brush my hair could be so... erotic. I was purring with pleasure by the time Glenn finished, stroking my hair to the side and kissing his way down my neck and back. He stopped his trail of kisses right above the curve of my ass, deciding to rub the mound of flesh instead, before pulling back and leaving me alone for a moment.

I was putty in his hand, his willing servant. Whatever Glenn had asked of me in that moment, I would readily do. But he didn't ask. He didn't want anything from me, besides for me to enjoy. He wanted to make my birthday special, and he had. We hadn't even done anything more than kiss a few times, and I already felt like the most precious person in the world. It was a heady sensation, and I was drowning in it.

Glenn returned, kissing his way up my legs, pausing to gently nibble my left cheek, before making his way up my body. I could feel him against me, the heat radiating from his skin without anything but his hands ever making contact with my body. And what hands they were. He rubbed some sort of oil or lotion into my skin, expertly working every muscle, every little knot, out. He kneaded and rubbed until I was so relaxed that I couldn't feel my toes, and then he rolled me to lay on my back, grinning down at me, and repeated the process on my front.

His touch was never sexual, it was soft when I needed soft, and firm when I needed firm, and always, always respectful. He knew I wanted him, I could see it in his eyes, but this was about me letting go and relaxing on my birthday, and later, his eyes promised, when I was free of the constant tension, we would give me what I had been asking for.

I never knew there were so many places to hide tension in my body. Whenever I thought of a massage, it was the back and shoulders, sometimes the legs or feet, but never the front. Never the abs, or the pectoral muscles, or the knees and shins. But Glenn massaged it all, working out knots that had knots, and cleansing my muscles that had never been touched by anyone but me of the tension they held so tightly.

By the time Glenn had finished, I felt like I was flying, basking in this pure, blissful relaxation.

When every bit of tension had left my body, Glenn bent forward, and he took possession of my lips. The kiss was slow and sensuous, awakening the fire in me that had been burning all night. I watched him through hooded eyes, waiting to see what he would do next once he pulled back. I knew better than to try and take control. This was Glenn's night to give me what I needed. There would be other nights for me to take and give.

We'd been forced to start the bond before we'd planned, but I would give him control of everything else it was within my power to give him. The shadows were spreading through him, even now, but I knew that he needed this, needed to be the one to choose how it would happen.

He stared down at me, his greedy eyes taking in every inch of my relaxed body, a soft smile gracing his lips as he looked his fill. I admired his sculpted physique. He looked like one of those statues of ancient gods come to life. My very own Adonis. I couldn't stop the smile that broke across my face at the sight of him, and when he chuckled, the sound filled with need, I didn't want to. I didn't want to hide any of my reactions to him, because Glenn deserved everything. He deserved every smile, every laugh, every gasp and moan and groan. And I planned to give it to him.

Something about the look in my eyes had his breath catching in his throat, a hunger overtaking his previous patience. He stalked forward, crawling languorously up my body, kissing and nibbling as he went. He was ravaging me, devouring me in a way that I never knew I wanted, but definitely knew, now that it was happening, that I needed.

I moaned as he sucked a sensitive nipple, rolling it around with his tongue.

"Glenn," I gasped as he fondled the other breast while teasing the nipple between his lips.

My hands fluttered around, wanting to grasp his head to my breast, but also wanting to let him have his way with me without me hands influencing his actions. The desire to let him explore won out, my hand falling to my sides and clenching the towels beneath us, twisting them in my fists as he explored my body with his expert hands and hot mouth.

By the time he made his way back up to my mouth, I was writhing with need, panting and begging him for more. He stared down into my eyes, a wide grin on his handsome face as he ran his hands up and down my sides, avoiding my most sensitive places.

"You're perfect," he said, his voice rough with need.

Finally, one of his hands moved between my legs, stroking along my seam as I struggled to keep from thrusting myself against him. Glenn chuckled darkly, dipping his head to kiss my neck again.

"You're so wet for me, Silver," he ground out, dipping one finger inside my slit and swirling it around, leaving me gasping at the new sensation.

More, I needed more. But I needed to look into Glenn's eyes as he explored my body more than I needed to fill that aching need, so I forced myself to still, gritting my teeth against the barrage of sensation and watching Glenn carefully.

He saw my struggle and smiled, kissing me gently before flicking my clit and chuckling when my whole body bucked against him, my restraint snapping at the delectable wave of pleasure that his motion sent rushing through me. I groaned into his mouth as he claimed my lips, working me into a frenzy before pulling back and licking my juices from his fingers, leaving me gasping in delight.

I was squirming with need as he positioned himself against my entrance, pausing and staring into my eyes. Unable to wait any longer, I growled and dug my fingers into his ass, jerking his lower half closer until he buried himself inside of me with a groan.

"Mine," I purred, yanking his head back down and crashing our lips together.

He moaned into my mouth, moving slowly in and out of me, the sensual pace driving me mad.

He pulled back from our kiss, nibbling his way up my neck, nuzzling a place just below my left ear and purring as our bodies came together rhythmically. I was lost to the sensations when his fangs gently scraped the sensitive spot, leaving me moaning for more. When he began to pull back, I grabbed his head and held him close.

"You will mark me," I growled into his ear, crashing my hip up against his, forcing him to quicken the pace.

He moaned, gently sinking his fangs into my flesh, sending me crashing into a wave of pleasure as he continued pumping into me. I moaned, shuddering with delight as he licked his mark.

I buried my hands in his hair, bending his neck back and licking my lips. I traced my tongue up along his collarbone, stopping at the juncture where his neck and shoulder merged and clamping down, my fangs burying themselves deep within his flesh, leaving him shuddering in delight as his motions became jerky.

He reached down, fumbling between us until he stroked my clit. I pulled my fangs from his neck, licking the puncture wounds and letting out a rough gasp as he tweaked my clit again, crashing our lips together and sending me shuddering over the edge of pleasure once more, my walls spasming and milking his cock as his motions stuttered to a jerky halt, Glenn collapsing on top of me, his breaths coming in shuddering gasps.

I frowned. Something wasn't right. I couldn't feel the mate bond snapping into place, despite the fact that we had mated and marked one another. Just as I was about to say something, the wave of power came rushing through me, the bond snapping into place as another earth-shattering orgasm ripped through me, Glenn's cry echoing my own as aftershocks of pleasure raced through us in a loop of increasingly intense delight that gradually faded, leaving me seeing stars.

"Wow," Glenn said when his jaw finally unclenched.

"Yeah," I replied, staring up into his eyes.

We sat there for a moment just basking in each other's presence, until Glenn grinned and scooped me up into his arms, stalking into the bathroom.

He tested the water of the tub, grinning before sliding me down into the now perfectly warm water.

"So that's why you made it so hot," I chuckled.

He nodded and slid in behind me, holding me to his chest.

"That was the best first time a guy could ask for," he murmured in my ear, making me gasp.

"That was your—"

"Yes. I wanted to wait for my mate. I wanted to make sure you had all of me," he said, kissing his mark, making me shudder in his arms.

He really was amazing.

I turned in his arms, staring into his eyes, looking for any hint of regret, or of that inky darkness. Finding neither, I relaxed, enjoying my mate.

Best. Birthday. Ever.

CHAPTER TWENTY-ONE

I was jerked out of my sex-induced haze the following morning by Blade knocking on the door.

"Hey lovers, hate to interrupt, but we have a situation." He shoved his head inside and flashed me a small smile. "Happy belated birthday, Everly."

I took a moment to stretch before flopping out of bed and tugging on the first things I grabbed. Glenn disappeared into his room, returning before I had even finished clasping my bra, to watch me dress with hungry eyes. We must've been up at least half the night, delighting in each other's bodies.

As much as I enjoyed our dalliance, I was regretting round three right about now. Glenn chuckled and kissed my cheek, sweeping me up into his arms once more and trotting down the stairs like a strutting peacock, stretching his neck to display his mark proudly.

Blade and Hunter grinned happily when they saw our matching marks, patting Glenn on the back before preparing me a plate of eggs and ham.

"No I do not like green eggs and ham," I muttered sarcastically as they preened.

Hunter heard me and snorted, shaking his head as his eyes gleamed with promise. Last night was about Glenn, but tonight was for me and Hunter, the gleam said. I wanted time with Blade, too, but I didn't want to push him into anything before he was ready, so instead of saying anything, I nodded discreetly at Hunter and turned to face Blade.

"What sort of situation?" I asked between mouthfuls of eggs.

He blew out a tired breath and filled me in. The Oberon had been spotted at the local elementary school run by the Shadow Keeper pack.

At least one child was missing. Despite the best efforts of the joint packs, nobody could find them or get in touch with their parents.

My stomach dropped at the news. I forced down the bite of eggs I had been chewing and pushed my plate away, lurching to my feet.

"We need to go," I declared, determined not to lose another person to the ravenous, monstrous shadows.

We piled into my SUV, Blade taking the wheel. It took about fifteen minutes to make our way to the elementary school, which was on the edge of the Shadow Keeper pack land and the neutral territory that made up most of the main town.

When we arrived, there was already a crowd of people, including my mates' parents and several enforcers from the various packs. We were greeted with worried frowns.

"There they are, thank the Goddess. Please, Watcher, alphas, you must help us," cried an elderly woman who I recalled from one of the Shadow Keeper pack runs that I had attended. She taught kindergarten at the pack school. Her face was fraught with worry, stress evident in her sunken eyes. She looked like she had aged years since I last saw her, just a few weeks ago.

"Tell us everything you know, Beverly," Hunter said. "We will fix this."

Her eyes hardened, her mouth dipping into a determined line as she explained what had happened.

The Oberon had been seen lurking near the edges of the school during recess, so the teachers herded all their students inside. Many of the children were hysterical, fear leaving them inconsolable. Once they managed to usher everyone inside and lock the school down, she and the other teachers took role while the administration alerted the packs of the threat. Two students were missing. They weren't in the bathrooms or in the wrong class, they were gone. A brother and sister that liked to play near the trees, they were the two that first noticed the threat, calling out the warning.

Beverly wasn't sure how they had gotten lost in the chaos, since they had been right beside her as they evacuated the children from the playground, but when roll was called, they were gone. Enforcers had scoured the forest, but couldn't locate the children. Beverly attempted to contact their parents, but was unable to get ahold of them, which led to Gerard sending enforcers to their home. They found the house empty, the place trashed, and the parents absent.

"Is there any trail?" Hunter demanded of the nearest enforcer.

"No, sir. The children's scent is along the edge of the forest, but disappears a few feet past the boundary."

Hunter frowned, glancing at me.

"Show me," I said, taking charge.

The enforcers glanced at their alphas briefly before doing as I requested. Most of the men here had attended one or more of our training sessions, and had some semblance of an idea of what I was capable of. Those who didn't followed the lead of the ones more familiar with me and my mates.

I was shown the place where the kids' scents disappeared and given an article of each of their clothes to help filter their scent out from the many overlapping smells littering the area.

"Do you have anything belonging to the parents?"

I was handed a scarf. It had a floral scent that I recognized as belonging to one of Moon Walker's omegas. I growled, recalling the sweet, helpful woman who showed me around the Moon Walker pack lands during one of my visits.

Once I had familiarized myself with all the scents, I handed the articles back to the enforcer who was shadowing me and stalked around, scenting the air.

It didn't take long to filter through the overlapping smells and identify the stench of the Oberon, which was masking the children's unique smells. I nodded towards my mates before taking off through the trees, my mates and the enforcers hot on my tail.

The trail led me deeper into the woods than I had been before, beyond the boundaries of any of the pack lands and into a wild, untouched part of the mountainous region we called home. I slowed, waiting for the other to catch up, when the scents grew thick in the air.

"Be alert," I murmured, glancing around. "This area reeks of Oberon."

Hunter, Glenn, and Blade surrounded me, looking around warily as I tried to weed through the crossing paths of scent trails. I was unable to pick up the scent of the Oberon that had the children, but the stench of fear mixed with the scarf owner's scent drew my attention to another trail that led deeper into the mountains.

"I lost the kids, but found their mom," I told my mates.

Hunter fell back, letting me take the lead once more as I followed the trail, stalking my way through the increasingly rocky terrain. The trail led us to a shallow cave, which was empty.

I frowned and looked around, sniffing the air. Blade poked around the walls, grunting and pulling against a loose rock.

The rock sprang back after he released it, a grinding sound emanating from the back of the cave. We watched warily as the rear wall of the cave slid into the ground to reveal a cavernous room, men and women in shackles dangling from the rough-hewn walls.

For something like this to be here, the Oberon had to be more sophisticated than we thought. I could see the concern echoes in Blade's eyes as he barked orders to the enforcing, instructing some to secure the area and others to release the prisoners.

There were ten people chained up in that cave, each one looking worse than the last.

"Please, no," whispered the Moon Walker woman whose scent had led us here.

"It's okay, Patricia," I whispered, recalling her name now that we were face to face.

"No, you don't understand," she choked out, gasping in pain as she was eased down.

"Tell me."

"The Oberon. They took us. We're infected," she sobbed, her voice cracking with her devastation.

I glanced at Blade, who hurried over.

"Do you think you can do it?" he asked softly.

We had been practicing using my light to pinpoint shadows and burn them away. We were sure we had perfected the technique when used on a Ghost Dancer or light-affiliated supernatural, but couldn't be certain if it would work on a Shadow-affiliated person without harming them. Since Patricia was Moon Walker, a gray pack member, we had a fifty-fifty chance of success.

I approached her, softly explaining the risks. She stared at me, her body shuddering as one of the enforcers helped her drink some water.

"Do it," she croaked. "The risk is…better than the alternative."

I nodded, gathering the light in my chest and placing my palms on her shoulders. I closed my eyes, not wanting to be distracted by our dismal surroundings. I gathered the light and gently eased it through our point of contact, slowly snaking it through her physical form. This was the first time I had done this on an actual person, and I knew that I needed to get it right, so when I located the place where her magic rested, I gently prodded it with my own.

It took some coaxing, but I was finally able to pinpoint where the shadows had latched onto her. Quick as a whip, I reached out with my light, caging the writhing darkness and burning it away. I was careful not to disturb more of her essence than absolutely necessary, worried about doing permanent damage.

When I felt the last of the shadows melt away, I drifted through the rest of her energy, searching for any wisp of that darkness, hiding away. When I didn't find any, I eased my energy back, sucking it back into my own body and deflating.

It took more out of me than I expected, but opening my eyes to find Patricia glowing with energy, the sallow look in her eyes replaced by the vitality that I had grown to expect, I knew it was worth it.

I was also able to confirm that Orin's words were true, the disease was siphoning the energy of its victims.

I glanced around at the others. We needed to help all of them, but this wasn't the time or place.

"Patricia, there's no easy way to tell you this. Your kids have been taken, do you know why? Or where they would take them?"

She looked at me in horror, tears filling her eyes. I sighed and waved the enforcer back over, having him take her back to pack lands until she could collect herself enough to help.

"We can't risk cleansing them all here," Blade murmured, echoing my thoughts.

"No, we can't. But I don't know if we can risk going back to help them right now. The moment the Oberon realize this group is missing, those kids are in more danger than before. Initially, they were just bait, but losing this source of power might make them the next meal."

Hunter nodded his agreement, waving one of his enforcers over.

"Take this group back to the pack. Keep them under constant watch. They're infected still, and until we have a chance to find those kids, we can't risk calling off the hunt."

With their marching orders in hand, twenty of the thirty enforcers with us took the infected back toward Shadow Keeper land. Hunter promised that his dad already had things set up for a potential situation like this.

We stalked out of the cave, searching for clues about where another stash like this might be, or where the children might have been taken.

"How long was Patricia gone?" I asked Glenn.

"Just today. She was at dinner with Mom and Dad yesterday."

I frowned, waving Hunter and Blade over.

"Did you guys recognize any of those people?"

"Yeah, a few," Blade confirmed.

Hunter nodded, a frown marring his face.

"When was the last time any of them were seen?"

"Last night, at the pack run," Hunter hissed, anger lacing his voice.

"Yeah, I saw those I recognized yesterday," Blade echoed.

"So sometime between last night and this morning, at least ten people were snatched and dragged here, infected with the Oberon, and left. Why? And how?"

"The real question is why they would pick up the children when they already had these guys?" Blade said uneasily. "That group packed a lot of power. If the one controlling them all really is siphoning the victims' strength, as it appears to be given the reaction we just saw when Everly burned the shadows from Patricia, then what use are the children?"

"A trap," Glenn stated grimly.

"If they're a trap to lure us out, does that mean they're safe for now?" Hunter wondered aloud.

"Maybe, if we hadn't released these ones," I waved towards the now empty cavern.

"What we should really be concerned about, is the level of sophistication this setup has," Blade said, sweeping his eyes round the cavern.

I nodded in agreement, glancing around. I wondered if some of those surrounding us might be infected too, and not even realize it. Not wanting to dwell on such morbid thoughts, I clapped my hands and stepped back, sniffing the air once more.

It took several circuits around the area before I picked the original scent back up. I followed it slower this time, not wanting to miss anything.

The sun was setting once more when I finally lost the scent. We were deep in the mountains, well beyond any of our pack lands, possibly beyond the bounds of the ley lines.

"Everyone spread out," Hunter shouted. "Look for another cave or something. We're looking for those kids. I don't want to go home without them."

The enforcers moved out immediately, searching every inch of space in the dim moonlight. I decided to shift, hoping the stronger senses of my wolf would be able to get us a more accurate location.

Hunter followed close behind as I paced around, nose to the rocky ground. After about fifteen minutes of back and forth, the wind shifted, bringing me a hint of the kids' scent. I resisted the urge to tip my head back and howl in favor of smacking Hunter repeatedly with my tail. He got the hint, waving Glenn and Blade over to follow me as I stalked through the craggy mountain bushes.

It was about 200 yards off the main goat tracks that we had been following that we found them, sleeping peacefully at the edge of a sharp cliff.

It was clearly a trap, so when Hunter and Blade scooped up the children, and no shadowy monsters jumped out to accost us, I was troubled.

I sniffed the children, inhaling deeply in search of that musky decay that accompanied the shadows. Nothing. I sent small feelers of magic creeping through their auras, also coming up empty.

Uncertain, I shifted back, glancing around.

"What's wrong?" Glenn asked, guiding me away from the cliff.

"Something doesn't feel right," I murmured, following their lead back towards the larger group. "We all know that their abduction was a trap, so why wasn't it sprung?"

Blade shook his head, marching back towards the enforcers and depositing the child on the ground before shifting.

"We're going to shift and run back, strap the kids to mine and Blade's backs and follow. Maintain a perimeter around us and keep your eyes open. This was too easy."

Once again, the enforcers moved without question, doing as they were told. I watched everything warily, not relaxing until we were back within the borders of pack lands, and even then, keeping my ears open for another ambush.

When nothing more happened, I was content to follow Blade and Hunter back to the Moon Walker packhouse, where Patricia and Gerard were waiting for us.

We carefully passed the children off, worries filling me at their stillness. They might not be infected, but something wasn't right. Something that we needed to get to the bottom of, and quickly.

CHAPTER TWENTY-TWO

I was beyond exhausted by the time we made it home, and much more worried than before. Glenn assured me that nothing more could be done tonight, which was the only thing that convinced me to sleep for a few hours. That and the knowledge that I'd be useless without rest.

When I awoke the next morning, Hunter was sitting at the table, nursing a cup of coffee and looking like he hadn't slept for days.

"What's wrong?" I asked, kissing his cheek and making myself a cup of tea.

Blade and Glenn came down while I was fixing my cup, each looking about as rested as Hunter did. I frowned, inspecting my mates with a critical eye before taking my place at the table and waiting for everyone to grab their drinks and sit.

The moment Glenn's ass grazed his seat, I was demanding answers.

"They never woke up," Hunter said, a shadowed look on his face.

"We can't find any hint of the Oberon in their bloodstream," Blade added, reminding me that he had told me his father was able to identify a protein in the infected that we had burned the shadows out of that wasn't present in anyone else.

"We confirmed that the test works on active infections," Glenn murmured between bites of cold, two-day-old pasta.

"So the kids aren't infected, but they haven't woken up. Has their energy been checked by someone a little more experienced than me? What about their father? Did Patricia have anything to add?"

"The local coven did a full battery of tests, as did the hospital. There is nothing magical or mundane that we can find wrong with them. Their father wasn't among those trapped in the cave, and Patricia has been too distraught to add much."

"The news isn't all negative, though," Blade added once Hunter was finished. "We've determined that the protein we've associated with the infection disappears after a while. The first group that you burned the shadows out of are showing results without it now, and some of them are regaining their memories. We think that the protein has something to do with how their memories are obscured."

"Can we use this information to identify who is infected? Give everyone a blood test?"

Blade grimaced. "I wish, but the resources needed to create the test are ridiculously rare. We could potentially, with time, mass produce the tests, but we're looking at a year or more lead time."

"Well, while we're all hoping to have the issue solved sooner than that, we should act like it won't be and put these contingency plans into motion."

Blade nodded his agreement, picking up his phone and sending a series of texts before looking back to me.

"What are the people who are regaining their memories saying?" I asked, a heavy weight on my chest.

"It's not good," Blade whispered, a broken look in his eyes.

"Tell me."

He shook his head.

"You need to go see them yourself. I can't convey what they did, and you need to see the full effect to understand."

"Alright, when do we leave?"

Hunter grunted, drawing my attention. He looked exhausted. They all did.

"Have we done everything we can for the kids?"

"Yes," Glenn said simply, a sad note in his voice.

"Alright. Then you three should get some rest. I'll go to the shop, and when you've all had some sleep, we can go talk to the... we can't keep calling them 'the first group.'" I frowned.

"The Burnt," Glenn said simply.

I nodded, that was as good a title as any. "Right. Once you've all gotten some sleep, we'll go interview the Burnt and see if we can piece a little more of this puzzle together."

They all agreed, dropping kisses on my head before disappearing into their rooms.

I putzed around the house, tidying up during the time that I would normally be training with Hunter, heading out right at half past nine to make it to the shop before opening.

When I arrived, Camille was already there, sweeping the cafe.

"Hey Cam, I'll be in my office," I told her, breezing by with barely a glance.

Her grunted agreement made me frown, but I was too focused on getting everything for the shop dealt with before I had to head over to visit the Burnt. I'd been dumping a ton of responsibility on Camille recently, and it was no wonder she was getting cranky about it. I'd have to talk with her once all this was over. She deserved a raise, at the very least.

It was nearly two by the time I came up for air, having managed to get everything entered into our old-fashioned excel spreadsheet that kept track of everything. I really needed to bring the shop into the modern world and get a proper inventory tracker going that could automatically scan and update whenever we sold something. I'd have to look into that another time, though, because Hunter had just texted saying they'd be by to pick me up in half an hour.

I closed up the ancient computer, slapped the ledger closed, and marched out of the office to find Camille slumped over at the checkout desk, looking a little green.

"Are you alright, Cam?"

She glanced at me, a miserable look upon her face and shrugged.

"Just a stomach bug," she grunted out, her voice coarse.

Something didn't sit right with me, but rather than push, I forced a sympathetic smile to my face and patter her shoulder. The moment my fingers connected, a static shock made me jump back with a yelp and a nervous laugh.

"Sorry," Camille muttered, "guess I'm a little shocking today." She tried to smile, but it looked more like a pained grimace.

"You should go home, Cam."

"But you have things to do," she protested. I felt a pang of guilt. I really *had* been dumping too much on her if she felt like my business came before her sickness.

"Being closed for a day or two isn't going to hurt. Your health is more important. Go home, get some rest."

She nodded stiffly, sliding off the stool and moving robotically towards the back to grab her things. I waited for Camille to limp out, watching as she shuffled down the street, disappearing around a corner before I locked the door, flipping the sign to closed.

Hunter pulled up a few moments later, driving Glenn's escalade.

"You boys feeling better?" I asked as I slid into the front seat.

"Much."

"Yep."

"Sure thing."

"Good," I said, some of the tension I had been holding onto since this morning draining out of me. At least they were okay. "Any news?"

"Nothing new. You ready to meet the Burnt?" Blade asked, his tone more somber than usual.

"Yeah, let's get this over with. The sooner we get all the pieces, the sooner we can solve the puzzle and fix this whole mess."

We drove in silence. I was somewhat surprised when we stopped outside the very hospital that I had been stuck in not too long ago.

"They're here?"

"Once the protein was out of their system, they no longer needed to be under guard."

"Do we think the protein impacts their ability to be controlled?"

"We're not certain, but it's a risk we didn't want to take. Until two days ago, they were in my packhouse's med bay," Hunter said simply.

I nodded my understanding, following as he led the way through the sterile halls of the Wolf Lake Regional Medical Center. We were admitted without issue, everyone dipping their heads in respect as we paced down the halls.

All three Elder Alphas met us outside the wing where the Burnt were being held, worried looks on all their faces.

"She should go in alone," Gerard said, pulling me in for a quick hug.

My mates offered feeble protests, but when their fathers all agreed with Gerard's assessment, they relented, hanging back to discuss the events of the past few days while I marched off, a sense of dread overtaking me as I entered the first room.

I interviewed seven people who had been in the first wave of Oberon to have the shadows burned out of them by my uncontrolled magic back in June. They all had similar things to say, most of which made my blood boil.

At first, they couldn't remember what had happened or where they were. They were confused, having lost days or weeks of time.

Their memories came back in spurts, a little here, a little there. They all recalled being forced to do terrible things, attack people close to them, drain magic from people, and funnel their shadowy disease into the hole made by taking that magic.

None of them wanted to do the things they were forced to do, each recalling having no control of their bodies when they refused orders.

None of them knew who was giving the orders. They rang through their minds, echoing like an alpha command during pack runs.

They were forced to prey on those closest to them, infecting dozens of people within the Ley Boundary and beyond. Each new revelation sent more anger rushing through me. Still, I kept on, asking the same questions, getting the same answers. They were beaten, abused, and manipulated. Their autonomy was stripped, and when they weren't being used, they were sent back into the world, stripped of the memories of the times they were under the influence of the shadows, living their lives as if nothing had happened.

It painted a terrible picture. People could be infected, spreading the disease, and not even realize it.

All of that was terrible, but it was the last one, the eighth person in that ward, whose words filled me with the most dread.

"I could feel him pulling at my soul," she said softly. "I thought, at first, that he was just drawing on me, but then I realized that he was using me—I was linked to my coven, and they to me, so by infecting me, he had access to all of our magic. He was siphoning them by controlling me, and I couldn't do anything about it."

The witch paused, staring blankly out the window.

"He's sick, that monster. He forced us to feed and infect others, and the strength we got from feeding he sucked right back out, taking a little more of us with him each time. The ones that were with him longer would succumb. I thought I'd be one. I was infected for a year. I don't know if he was more careful with me, or I was stronger than the others, or something else. My coven, perhaps."

She shook her head, taking a shuddering breath.

"He tries to get the strong ones when they're weak, targeting them just before their power blossoms. The few who can resist the compulsion are chained and beaten. He feeds on their fear and their pain. I don't know what he is... or rather, what he was, before he consumed the Darkness."

She glanced at me, her eyes focusing briefly before her gaze lost its clarity once more.

"He had her there, you know," she whispered.

"Had who where?"

"The Watcher." She glanced at me once more before chuckling darkly. "I guess she's not The Watcher anymore. That's you now, isn't it? She's so strong, I don't know how she's held on this long, or how much longer she can withstand his special attention."

She shuddered, shaking her head. "You must hurry."

"I don't understand, who is she?" I asked, dreading the answer.

Her eyes cleared once more as she stared at me, seeming to look into my very soul.

"Eustice, of course."

My heart stuttered. I stared at her through wide eyes, sheer shock the only thing that kept me from shaking the frail woman and demanding she make everything make sense. I took three deep breaths, closing my eyes and making sure I was fully in control of myself before I spoke, my words slipping out in a shaky whisper.

"Are you saying that Eustice Cummings, the previous Watcher, is still alive and trapped within the Oberon?"

She looked at me, that haunting clarity lashing me to my core.

I knew what she was saying, and she knew I knew. I just wanted her to say it, or rather, to say that it wasn't. She didn't, she just stared at me, willing me to understand, to see, and to accept what had been right in front of me all along.

I blew out another breath and nodded.

"Do you know where she's being kept?"

She shook her head, looking back out the window.

"I had no sense of direction when he was in control. I couldn't find the place where I was kept even if I tried. I can tell you that there were dozens of them, though. Little caves scattered all about. Some were connected in this network, but most weren't. Not long before you burned the shadows out of us, I heard him whispering about 'using the light.' He kept rambling on about binding souls with the light. I think he was looking to bind people without infecting them, so he could have an endless supply of power as long as their bodies remained alive. It's dark, dark magic that requires the purest of magics, and souls, as a sacrifice."

She shivered in disgust, shaking her head like she was trying to dislodge the insidious knowledge. I was horrified, but her words clicked with something inside of me.

The night that Glenn and I were attacked, one of the shadows had seemed to be draining my magic, absorbing the light that I used to burn the dark disease out of people. And then the next day, the children were abducted. Now they couldn't be woken.

I shuddered at the thought of those poor kids having their souls bound for some sick monster to gather more power.

"How would we break something like that?" I asked in a shaky voice.

She watched me closely, frowning.

"He did it," she stated, a mix of awe and horrified repulsion in her voice.

"I think so," I whispered.

She growled and sat up further in her bed.

"The only way to break a binding like that would be to destroy the anchor."

"What's the anchor?"

"I don't know. Find Eustice, she might know."

"Where's Eustice?"

"I don't know that, either," she growled in frustration.

I deflated, knowing that I wouldn't get anything more out of her.

Whatever was on my face when I made it back to my mates had them glancing at each other in worry.

"I think I know what's wrong with the kids," I whispered brokenly. "My magic did this."

CHAPTER TWENTY-THREE

I was in shock, I knew. Everything was numb, and all that was left was a broken husk. At least, that was how it felt.

My mates took me home, tucking me into bed. I didn't know how to fight the kind of evil that could steal the souls of children. How do you fight when the very power you use to do so is being ripped from you and manipulated to hurt more people?

You don't, I told myself.

Treoirn snorted, making me wince.

Will you give up so easily, Gaelana?

What's the point in fighting when I'm just going to give him what he needs? He'll just keep hurting them.

Did it ever occur to you that things tend to get harder when you're moving in the right direction?

I grimaced at her words. That couldn't be right, could it? She felt my crumbling resolve, and pressed on.

He's growing desperate, grasping at different ways to retain his power. You've dealt him serious blows, and as you tie your mates to you, you all grow stronger.

Do you really think that?

I know it, Gaelana. He's weakened. Each time you cleanse the shadows from another infected, it takes a slice of his strength. These are the actions of a desperate man, afraid of losing the power he unjustly stole from others.

Her words resonated within me, the truth of them giving me hope.

We could end him, we just needed... something.

I frowned, robotically eating my lunch while my mind whirred with everything I had learned.

How did I stop him? Burning the shadows was working to weaken him, but it drained me, leaving me unable to function. He was infecting people as faster than I could free them. I needed a way to stop him from draining people altogether. A way to deal a blow that weakened him enough for us to find and put a stop to the threat. If I could cut off his source of power, maybe we'd stand a chance.

But how?

I closed my eyes, thinking.

'Help us. Save us,' the whispering words from my dream flittered through my mind, jolting me.

The cave. I needed to find that cave, and that crystal. I needed to destroy that damn crystal. I knew that, somehow, it was the source of his power.

I glanced around, noticing for the first time that my mates had left me at home to go about their days.

I huffed out a breath. I should call them.

But what if they try to stop me? This needs to happen.

We should trust our mates, Gaelana.

I pushed Treoirn's concerned words down, relegating her to that corner in my mind where I hid all my worries, along with the treacherous little voice that reminded me how I'd felt when *I'd* been the one being sidelined.

I stepped outside, gazing at the mountains in the distance. Somewhere out there, was a network of caves with a lake of souls, hiding the source of the Oberon's power. I needed to find it.

I strode into the trees, letting my instincts guide me. My determination carried me on when my body wanted to stop. I didn't know where I was going, but I knew that I had to keep moving. Something was drawing me forth, and I had this wriggling thought that it was that cave. That crystal. Those trapped souls, begging for release.

And I was the only one who could free them. And maybe, just maybe, by freeing them, I could free the children too.

I marched on.

The sun had long since set by the time I reached the mountains, leaving a chill that was settling into my skin. The first snow of the season would be coming soon, but I could only hope that it wasn't tonight. I still had a long way to go, I knew.

My feet moved robotically, pushing me inexorably forward.

When I stopped before a yawning cavern, shivers racing through me, I knew I had found the entrance I had been looking for. I glanced back, trying to discern the path I had taken, but there was nothing to indicate where I had been.

I took a moment to look around, frowning at the realization that I had no clue where I was. The moon was high in the sky, giving no hint as to which way was east and which west. I shook the worry from my mind and pulled my phone from my pocket, holding it up.

No signal.

What did you expect, Everly? You're in the middle of nowhere, I berated myself.

I shook the worries off and straightened my shoulders, getting ready to march into the cave.

A scratching in my mind gave me pause. I tilted my head, trying to figure out what it was, when I realized with horror that I had pushed Treoirn so far back that she couldn't speak.

I hastily tossed open the mental cave I had shoved her in, ready to apologize when her voice rang out in my mind, a wild panic making me jerk back.

Everly watch out! she shouted, throwing herself against the walls of my mind, trying to break free from the chains that were still binding her.

Why were chains binding her? Why was she so far back in my mind? Wait, why was she panicking?

A shiver of unease raced through me as I stepped slowly back from the cave. Something was wrong.

I glanced around with dawning horror as I realized I was surrounded. Misshapen shadows were everywhere, moving silently around me.

I swallowed nervously, wondering what the hell I was thinking to come here alone. I carefully moved, one slow step at a time, trying to retrace my path back down the mountain.

It was the souls, Treoirn said sadly. *They are growing more desperate. When you dreamed of them, they must have left a tether to lead you back in your waking time.*

Are they trying to harm us?

No, but all they understand is their own desperation.

Are they in there? I asked, glancing at the cave.

Yes.

My foot landed on a dry piece of wood, the cracking of my weight settling on it echoing throughout the previously silence mountain range. I paused, hoping the shadows wouldn't react, but they all snapped their gazes toward me. Their hungry gazes.

I didn't know if these were people, or animals, or something else entirely. They didn't seem to notice me when I was in that trancelike state, but now, they had definitely noticed me. And I was dinner.

I moaned with fear, trying to call on my light. Treoirn was still fighting those damn chains, though, and before I could use the light, I had to free her. But I had to concentrate for that.

Why are you chained? I growled internally, still slowly backing away from the cave.

The shadows seemed almost like they were guarding it. I could see the hunger in their fiery gazes, but they didn't move to attack me as long as I was moving away from the cave. I wanted to test my theory, but until I had my wolf free, it was too much of a risk.

I don't know. I was just pushed to the back of your mind until we reached the mountains. It's like you triggered a ward of some sort that bound me.

That wasn't good. Did the monster controlling the shadows have that kind of magic? Or was he controlling witches, forcing them to create wards against their will?

I shivered. I didn't like the sound of either option.

As I backed up further, I felt a shiver of magic race over me. It made me pause, glancing up to watch the shadows' reactions.

They had started inching forward. I kept backing away, yanking at the chains binding Treoirn.

Another dozen or so yards, and we passed through another wave of magic, the chains shattering. But the shadows' restraint seemed to shatter with them, and the moment both my feet had crossed that invisible boundary, they all exploded forward, racing towards me.

Slow retreat wasn't working. I turned to race away as fast as I could while trying to call on my light.

It was sputtering, like the chains that had bound Treoirn were also draining my magic away.

As if a bad situation couldn't get any worse, my foot caught on a root just as I was gaining some distance between me and my pursuers.

"Shit, shit, shit, shit," I chanted as I flipped over and backed away, crab-walking backward.

I needed to get back to my feet, but I could barely move.

Just as the shadows were descending upon me, a light burst forth from the trees at my back. It landed just before me, spreading and growing until there was a wall of blinding white light between me and the shadows.

It was eerie how silent they were. I expected them to growl in anger at being blocked from their meal, but there was no sound at all. I could see through the light, but just barely.

What I saw made no sense. There were faces, like in that lake with the souls, writhing through the shadows with gaping mouths. I frowned, watching as they just... retreated. They slowly turned and marched back up the mountain, never looking back. None of it made sense, but I couldn't worry about that right now.

I turned, searching for the source of the light. Nothing appeared to me until the shadows were gone, beyond the ridge of the mountain.

I managed to stand and brush myself off before the wall of light faded, revealing the empty forest around me.

"Which way is home, Treoirn?"

She snorted and dipped her head to my left. I nodded and began marching in that direction, yelping in fear when a hand touched my shoulder.

I spun, dropping low and whipping my foot out with a growl, just as the person jumped back and held their hands up in a gesture of peace.

The haze of fear cleared, allowing me to think clearly for a moment. It was Orin.

"What are you doing here?" I demanded, willing my racing heart to calm the fuck down.

"Saving you from being dinner, apparently."

"The light was you?"

"Yes. I can't attack them directly because of the... But I can defend people."

It made sense. The geas seemed to prevent him from action directly against the so-called 'king' who controlled the shadows, in words or actions.

"Thanks for saving me. But that still doesn't explain why you're here."

"I was scouting. Searching for..."

"Ophelia? Lucille?"

His eyes widened in shock at my words.

"Apparently I sometimes get visions. Not enough to know the full story, but I know that you tried to trade yourself for the two of them, but when the shadows didn't take, the man who controls them took the two women and ran off."

He looked pained by the reminder, but I couldn't keep dancing around the truth. I needed to know what was going on.

He shook his head and held out his hand.

"We should get you home."

"As long as you can walk and talk, Orin. I need more information."

"Right."

He blew out a frustrated breath, rubbing his temples while he thought. After a moment, a light entered his eyes.

"I might be able... I'm going to tell you a tale, Everly."

I nodded. If he thought this would let him work round the geas, I was game.

"Once, long ago, before the ley line created the places of profound magic we know today as Ley Bound areas, there was a veil. This veil separated the magic from the mundane, offering safety to those who were persecuted by humans, those who held magic in their blood. The land on the other side of the veil was ruled by a King and Queen. Her name was Titania, and his…" he paused, as if testing whether the geas would react.

When it didn't, he continued.

"His name was Oberon. He was the king of the fae. Titania was like a golden goddess, all light and purity and happiness. Oberon was her counterpoint, a dark, brooding man. He was a kind and fair king, however, despite the darkness that lived inside of him. They had two children." Orin looked away, staring at the moon.

"Their eldest was a boy, they named him Orin. He took after his mother, all of her light in him. The second child was a girl, they named her Ophelia. She had the same dark magic as her father, but with the happy disposition of Titania. She was a bright spot in the court of the fae."

"Things were fine for millennia, the peace unprecedented. Unfortunately, as tends to be the way with all good things, the peace came to an end. The veil had been damaged, the magic of the different realms leaking into one another, corrupting one another, especially the realm of the mundane. You see, the realm of the mundane always had illnesses not seen elsewhere. Whereas the Magic Born, those born with any magic in their veins, tended to be immune to the sickness and diseases of the human realm, when the veils dropped, the magic of the other realms merged with some of those illnesses. It created diseases that could harm Magic or Mundane, ravaging through kingdoms and lands that had only been myth to the mundane world."

I had a sinking feeling that I knew where this was going.

"One such disease was called the Darkness. It came and wiped out much of the population of the fae kingdom, spreading like wildfire. Titania saw the sickness and sought to contain it. She found a way to burn it from the infected, leaving them immune, for a time. Her light was the only thing that worked, but it caused irreparable harm to those who were born in shadow, those who had darker magics were often left almost mundane themselves after the sickness had been purged from their systems. It left Oberon impotent with rage. He was infuriated that such a sickness was essentially targeting those like him, so he went off, seeking a more permanent solution."

Orin blew out a sad breath.

"Somewhere along the way, Oberon's mission changed. He no longer wanted to eliminate the disease, having realized that the strength it granted the infected who fed could be used to protect his kingdom, if only it could be controlled. Titania warned against such actions, promising that nothing came without a price, but Oberon was too stubborn to listen. He made his way to the mundane realm, where the Darkness had originated, and he sought the source. Eventually, he found it, deep in the mountains of this area. And then he found one of many caverns where great power resided. The Darkness was coming from the greed of humans as they hunted the native creatures of this land, wolves, elk, bears, buffalo. They took and took, finding ways to channel the magic in their pelt. The greed was so potent that it manifested the malevolent energy which latched on to one of their diseases, and it changed it."

He paused, staring into my eyes, willing me to understand.

"Oberon discovered all of this, and when he found that cave, and the power within it, he knew he could use it to control the disease. He bound the source of the sickness to a crystal within a cavern, and he used that to absorb the power gained by the infected who fed. Titania and Orin tried to stand against him, tried to convince him that he was making a mistake, but he was so filled with rage that his own flesh and blood, his own mate, would stand against him, that he cursed them. He made them impotent, unable to stand against him themselves. Of course, he thought that they were the only beings in existence with the strength and will to stand against his new weapon, but when he found that there was another clan, the Moon Clan fae who had fled the fae realm centuries prior to the collapse, he began to have them hunted."

I was horrified by Orin's tale, but I knew that he was giving me some vital information.

"Are there others who could stand against him that just won't?" I asked.

Orin's jaw clenched. He couldn't answer. I changed tactics.

"That's quite the tale. This cavern, it sounds suspiciously like the Cavern of Souls from Greek mythology."

"That's probably because it is. It's one of many."

"Would destroying that crystal create repercussions?"

He shrugged.

"Thank you for the story. I'll keep it in mind."

"Of course, Everly. Also keep in mind that your power grows as your mates are bound."

I nodded, making my way out of the trees and back towards the house alone. Quite the tale, indeed.

CHAPTER TWENTY-FOUR

I was only a little surprised to find Hunter waiting for me on the porch swing, a scowl on his face.

"Where have you been?" he demanded, making me bristle.

"I was running," I told him testily.

He growled, stalking towards me and crowing me.

"If you were just going for a run, why do you smell like fear?"

I flinched, pushing past him and grabbing a muffin. I was ravenous.

"Dammit, Everly! You disappeared again!" he shouted, making me frown.

"Well, yeah, generally when you don't know where someone is, that's an apt descriptor."

He took a ragged breath, his eyes flashing. When he spoke again, all his rage had deflated out of him, leaving only his terrified, broken voice.

"No, Everly," he whispered, "I mean," he touched his chest, "you were gone. The bond was gone. You left me."

I gasped, dropping my muffin. He bent to pick it up, handing me a fresh one while avoiding my gaze.

"Hunter, I'm so sorry. I didn't know."

He shook his head and pulled me to him, holding me tightly against his chest.

"I've been so worried. You were gone for hours."

I frowned. Hours? I couldn't have been within the range of those wards around the cave for more than thirty minutes or so. It must be something else interfering with the bond.

The souls, Treoirn whispered in my mind.

That made sense. They seemed to be influencing me, pulling me toward the cave. Maybe they blocked the bond.

Rather than tell Hunter all of this, I held him close, reassuring him that I was alright.

He pulled back, staring down at me.

I reached up and pulled his head down, bringing his lips to mine.

He kissed me with all of the desperation inside of him, like he couldn't breathe unless he tasted me again.

It wasn't long before I decided that he needed me more than any one or thing else in this moment, and brushed all of my worries and discoveries aside, focusing all of my attention on him.

I pulled back, staring into his eyes and stroking his cheek gently.

"I'm here, Hunter. I'm fine, and I'm not going anywhere," I reassured him softly, kissing each of his fingers before taking his hand and leading him upstairs.

He was hesitant, touching me almost like he was afraid I would break, or perhaps just fade away before his eyes.

I guided his hands along my body, up and down my sides, and under my shirt, reassuring him that I was here, and that I was real.

He dropped to his knees before me. I just stood there, letting him work his emotions out while I ran my hands through his hair. The front door opened and closed while we stood there, Hunter's arms wrapped around my waist and his head bowed.

Glenn peaked into the room, a worried look on his face. When he saw me, he smiled softly and retreated, gently closed the door behind him.

I briefly wondered if he had felt the same absence that had Hunter so worried, but quickly drew my attention back to Hunter, gently massaging his scalp. I would check on Glenn later. Right now, Hunter needed me.

When the constant shaking eased, I carefully unraveled his arms and kneeled before him. I moved slowly, stroking his face and tilting it so I could look into his eyes. He looked devastated, and I kept doing it to him, which was horrifying. I never wanted to hurt this man. Ever.

I gently kissed his lips, then his cheeks, nose, eyelids, and forehead. He gradually relaxed as I peppered him with small tokens of my affection, wanting to make sure he knew just how much I loved and needed him.

"I'm sorry I scared you, Hunter," I told him softly, resting our foreheads together. "I love you, I hope you know that. I would never intentionally cause you pain."

He smiled, the look a sad reflection of the smirks he usually gives.

"I know, little mate," he whispered, pulling my lips against his once more.

He deepened the kiss, groaning into my mouth. I was relieved that he seemed to be coming out of his stupor.

His hands worked their way down my neck, stroking their way past my shirt to dip down into the waistband of my pants as he tugged me closer.

He reached one hand back up to angle my head, keeping the other planted on my ass, holding us together securely.

My hands explored him.

I would never get enough of this man. He was all hard muscle and strength, hiding the most kind, funny man. He was so strong, his personality and emotions both, and he didn't try to hide either from me. It was intoxicating, knowing that he was all mine.

I stroked my way down his back, grasping his ass and squeezing just enough to let him know that I was more than ready to let him have his way with me.

He groaned, pulling back, panting. I licked my lips at the sight of his swollen lips, making him growl.

His eyes were hot and fierce as I slowly tugged my shirt off, enjoying the sound of his ragged breaths. He needed me as much as I needed him.

I disrobed, shaking my body and dancing just enough to have his eyes roving my body, his cock twitching beneath the layers of his clothes.

I grabbed the collar of his shirt, leading him towards the bed, where I pushed him down and straddled his body. His strangled moan filled me with a fierce pride, a sense of power.

All that strength, and he was completely under my spell. He tilted his head up, taking one of my nipples in his mouth and branding me with his hot tongue.

I reached my hands down while he lavished me with attention, sliding them under his shirt and relishing the feel of his muscles, which jerked at my every touch. I slowly pulled back, tugging his shirt up. He sat up, supported my weight, and helped me remove the offending fabric. I needed to touch him, to see him.

He growled when I pulled back, making me chuckle. I leaned forward and nibbled his ear, waiting until his hands went limp and his cock was straining against his jeans to pull back and drop to my knees before him.

Tonight was about Hunter.

I reached forward, trailing my fingers along the zipper of his jeans, enjoying the sight of his bulge twitching. I carefully unbuttoned his pants and lowered the zipper, pulling his delicious length free. I could help him take his pants off, but I decided on a different path instead, my mouth watering with the need to taste him.

His eyes widened as I took the tip of his cock into my mouth, groaning at the salty taste. He hissed as I swirled my tongue along the lower edge of his bulbous head, humming with delight. I reached my hands into his pants, cupping his balls, feeling their weight and tugging gently on them.

He was perfect.

I sucked him deeper, moving one of my hands to grasp his base, moving in time with my mouth, while the other continued to fondle his sac. I gently scraped my teeth along the top of his length as I pulled off, only to swirl my tongue along his tip and trace the bulging line below the head of his cock. He groaned, trying to pull me up, but I was relentless, wanting to taste him.

I could feel him growing, his cock twitching with the need to release its load, when he yanked me off of him, flipping us over and burying himself inside me in one smooth motion.

I groaned at the sudden sensation. He stretched me so perfectly, giving me a moment to adjust before he began pounding inside of me.

"Hunter," I moaned.

He reached down and rubbed my clit, circling it teasingly before gently flicking it in time with his thrusts. When he leaned down and licked his mark, I couldn't hold back, waves of ecstasy racing through me as I screamed in pleasure. Hunter groaned, pumping once, twice more, before shuddering, his motions stuttering as he collapsed on top of me, panting.

He rolled us over, holding me to his chest and kissing my head.

"I love you, Everly," he whispered before his eyes slid closed.

"I love you too, Hunter," I said, stroking his peaceful face.

I needed to tell him, tell all of them, about what Orin told me, but it could wait until morning.

I curled up against his chest and drifted off to sleep.

The morning came quickly enough, and after a quick shower, I raced downstairs to find all three of my mates sitting at the kitchen table, discussing the events of the past week.

"Good morning, mates," I said cheerily as I made my tea. It was a raspberry-peach kind of morning, I decided after a moment's contemplation.

Glenn, ever the caretaker, made me some yogurt with fruit and granola while I waited for my tea to steep. They continued their conversation, pausing only long enough to greet me and ensure I had breakfast.

I was happy, and peaceful. Until I wasn't. Glenn's mention of the bond dropping off last night snapped me out of my happy haze.

I cleared my throat, making them pause. They glanced at me, each with some variation of expectation on their face.

"Last night, I went for a run. I got lost and ended up in the mountains," I murmured, fudging the truth a bit. "Something there—a ward, I think—bound my wolf and my powers. I think that's why the bond dropped off."

Glenn and Hunter frowned, while Blade looked contemplative.

"There were shadows there, but they didn't attack. It was like they were guarding something. I think the cave we need is somewhere up there."

Blade nodded.

"That would make sense with what I've found. What else?"

"When I retreated past the ward, they chased me, but they waited until I had completely crossed the boundary."

"Could you find the place again?" Glenn asked, sharing a look with Hunter.

"I'm not sure, but I didn't get away on my own, guys. Orin appeared, and he told me a story as he escorted me home."

"Stories don't help us," Hunter muttered sulkily.

Blade shot him a look while Glenn patted his shoulder. I just rolled my eyes and continued on.

"This one might. Did you know that Oberon is the name of the last Fae King?"

That got their attention.

"Apparently, Oberon is also the name of Orin's father. His mother is called Titania. Orin takes after his mother, who has light magic. He has a sister named Ophelia," I said, willing them to remember our discussion about my last dream.

"That's in line with the vision you had," Blade said softly.

I nodded before pressing on.

"Apparently, there also used to be something called the veil? It kept magic out of the human realm. When it dropped, certain human diseases mutated."

"That's all mentioned in some of the ancient texts I found, but I had to do a lot of digging to find it."

I was relieved by Blade's confirmation. If that much was true, then surely the rest of Orin's tale was as well. Which meant it contained the hints we needed to finally end this war with the Oberon. King Oberon. The last Fae King, driven mad with power.

I told them the rest, about how Oberon was angry with the disease, how he learned to channel the power boost it gave its victims, and how he refused to stop, binding his wife and children with a geas when they dared to suggest he quit his mad quest. My mates' faces moved through a range of emotion, from understanding to rage and back again.

When I finally finished, they sat there in stunned silence, processing my words.

"This fills in a lot of gaps," Blade finally said.

"Yeah. We're still missing a lot of information, though," I muttered, taking a spoonful of my yogurt. My eyes widened as the taste it hit my tongue. Glenn smirked and wiped an escaped bit of the deliciousness from my lips before facing Blade once more.

"Does this give you enough of a starting point to find the rest of the answers we need?" he asked Blade, who nodded thoughtfully.

"I'll head to the library and get started. You should head to the shop, Everly. I heard that Camille isn't feeling well."

"No, she looked a little green yesterday," I said.

"I have to go help with the hunt," Hunter muttered, glaring at his toast.

"What hunt?"

"We're searching for more caves like that one. Another dozen or so people were noticed as having disappeared in the last two days."

"That's horrible. Do you need me to come burn the shadows?"

"Not yet. I'll let you know when we're ready."

"I'll be ready," I promised. *Somehow.*

CHAPTER TWENTY-FIVE

For once, it was an uneventful day. I worked at the shop, starting the arduous process of getting a proper inventory system setup, and then rode home with Glenn.

When we got home, my happy day was shattered.

The front door to my house, our house, was broken, hanging half off its hinges. Glenn and I stepped up to the porch and inspected the damage.

It looked like someone had a fight on my front porch. There was dirt scattered about, and bloody handprints on the broken door. We followed a trail of blood and dirt inside, finding a crumpled body in the middle of the kitchen.

I gasped when I recognized Camille crumpled on my kitchen floor, her small frame curled into a writhing ball. She moaned as we approached.

I wanted to roll her over, but didn't want to hurt her. I glanced at Glenn, my eyes begging him to do something to fix this. He had his phone to his ear and was whispering furiously, so I turned back to Camille to try and comfort her. He was probably calling an ambulance or something. He would know what to do, how to handle this.

Camille stilled for a moment before moaning, the sound rife with pain, and curling into a tighter ball.

"Cam, Cammy, Camille," I chanted her name as I stroked her hair.

She was in no condition to respond. I wondered briefly if this had to do with her being sick the other day.

Or maybe it has something to do with why Orin ran out after he saw her, I thought bitterly.

She arched her back suddenly, almost hitting me in the face. I took the opportunity to roll her onto her back, gasping at the sight before me.

There were black streaks running through her veins, looking like poison. It looked like shadows crawling through her bloodstream. I swallowed, wondering if I should use my magic to try and isolate whatever it was, but quickly dismissed the thought. Without knowing what was wrong or how to fix it, I might make things worse by just flinging magic around.

I ground my teeth and held her still as her body convulsed. It looked like she was having a seizure, but not any kind of seizure I had ever seen.

She screamed, the sound making my chest ache, it was so filled with agony.

"I'm so sorry, Cam," I said, grabbing her wrists as she tried scratching at her face.

It was like she was trying to peel her skin off. I didn't want her to hurt herself, so I held her wrists down, glaring at Glenn as he hung up the phone and kneeled beside me, a worried frown on his face.

"What's wrong with her?" I asked through gritted teeth.

He shook his head and peeled back her eyelid, his lips thinning at the sight beneath. Her eyes were pure black. Not just the iris, but the whole eye, the white, the iris, the pupil, they were all pitch black. Like the Oberon. No, the Darkness. Oberon was just the monster controlling it. He did this, I knew. He was sending me a message that no one was safe.

Shadows lashed at my hands, forcing me to yank them back as pain like a thousand needles scraping my skin. I watched in horror as the shadows climbed up Camille's body. She clawed at her throat, gasping for breath.

The darkness in her eyes parted briefly as the shadows engulfed her, showing me a glimpse of her terrified, agonized face, bloody tears leaking from her eyes just before the shadows consumed them, and then her, completely.

Glenn growled, grasping at Camille as she jumped up and hissed, the sound sending chills racing down my back.

"Cam, no, stop, we can help!" I shouted as she backed away towards the rear door.

She shook her head, making me think there was still a piece of her in there, then turned and darted out the door and into the woods.

I raced after her.

She was fast. Too fast. I could barely keep her in my line of sight. We raced through the trees, the shadowy Camille ducking and dodging faster than I had ever seen her move before. It was terrifying, the realization that the darkness gave everyone it touched a boost, when that extra energy wasn't being drained by Oberon. If he just left it be, he would have an unstoppable army. I could only hope that he never realized that. And that if he did, Cam wouldn't be caught up in his sordid plans. We had to find a way to help her.

I. *I* had to find a way to help her.

And I would.

I raced through the trees, keeping her just in my line of sight. I was panting by the time she began to slow, my mind whirring with options on how to save her. I wouldn't let her stay like this, controlled by a madman.

I recognized the place she had begun to slow as the border between the forest and the mountain where Orin had found me the night before. It couldn't be a coincidence that Camille was drawn here. But was it to try and trap me, or was she disobeying orders by coming to me before Oberon could wipe her memories? Was his plan to use her as a spy?

I didn't know, and I couldn't slow down long enough to find out. I had to save her.

Her movements changed once we crossed into the mountains, moving from the smooth gait of a shifter to a robotically stiff shuffling, like the last piece of her had fallen away, leaving nothing more than a husk in Oberon's control.

She stopped, turned, and release an ear-splitting screech. It was an inhuman sound that literally made my ears bleed. I reached up to touch my face when liquid began dripping down to find my nose bleeding as well.

That was new, and not at all welcome.

Shadows flooded from everywhere, surrounding me. I twirled around, unable to keep my focus on just one. They flooded around me in a never-ending stream, parting like the sea for a larger, darker shadow. That had to be Oberon. Thanks to Shadow Camille's shriek, I couldn't tell if he was speaking, trying to scare me once more. My ears were ringing. I tried not to take my eyes from Oberon, but a movement behind him drew my attention, and my gasp.

Wolves were streaming from the trees and the craggy mountains, surrounding the shadows. I didn't know where they had come from, but I was grateful for their presence.

Hunter, Glenn, and Blade soared over the shadows, their wolfy faces snarling as they circled me. I had forgotten all about Glenn, too focused on trying to save Camille. He must've been speaking to one of my other mates when he was on the phone, calling for backup. I was glad that one of us had some sense.

The ringing in my ears was starting to clear, leaving me unfortunately able to hear Oberon's hissing laugh.

"The game is up, Oberon," I shouted, much to his delight.

"Oh, no, the game has just begin, Moonchild."

I summoned a ball of light and lobbed it at him, but he just swatted it aside like a pesky bug. How the fuck did Orin expect me to stop his father if he was this strong? I growled, changing tactics. I began to toss my light into the crowd of shadows, willing it to burn the sickness out of them. Most of those it touched fell to their knees, squealing as the shadows were peeled away, before passing out.

Oberon growled, lunging towards us, only to be stopped by a wall of light. I looked around, searching for Orin, but he was nowhere to be found.

I recalled him telling me that he couldn't act directly against his father, but he could protect people from him.

Oberon snarled and slammed his fist against the wall, creating fissures. Desperately, I gathered as much light as I could, and pushed it at him. It began eating away at the shadows clinging to him, revealing the imposing man from my dreams, a terrifying sneer on his face.

"This isn't over, Moonchild," he snarled, slamming his fist against the wall and shattering it.

Hunter jumped in front of me, nipping at the man's feet and forcing him to retreat.

"You'll never save the old lady, Moonchild. She's mine," he hissed before turning and racing off into the mountains.

Several enforcers moved to follow him, but were blocked by some of the larger shadows who I couldn't cleanse. I resumed throwing my light at the remaining shadows, but it grew less and less effective. I growled in frustration as another screech sounded, this one lower in pitch, and the remaining shadows just... popped out of existence.

I fell to my knees and checked over each of my mates, making sure they weren't hurt. There was blood on them, but none of it was theirs.

Reassured, I waited for them to shift back before wading through the unconscious people on the ground, searching for Camille.

She wasn't there. I leaned my head back and howled, the sound a haunting echo from my human throat. The wolves around me responded, singing a song of loss and impotent anger.

Orin stepped from behind the trees, a grim look on his face.

"Now that he knows you've seen the truth, he's going to get worse," he warned.

"He has Camille," I growled. And I couldn't just leave her to his manipulations.

Orin nodded. "She was already infected the first day. She was fighting it better than most. I believe she may have been placed under a geas because of her resistance."

His words made my chest ache. Poor Camille. She'd been targeted because of me. I couldn't let this go on.

"We have to stop him."

"I've helped all I can," Orin said sadly.

"I know. Thank you."

He glanced around, inspecting each person around us and leaning closer.

"There are no more active infections here, but beware, your friend won't be the only pawn that he has selected. He didn't hold the throne for thousands of years without being cunning."

I nodded and squeezed his hand in thanks, waving my mates over.

"This is Orin."

"We've met," Hunter said.

"It's nice to see you again, Prince Orin," Blade said mildly.

"Thanks for looking after our mate," Glenn nodded.

They talked amongst themselves briefly before Orin retreated, melting into the trees.

"He's going to look into the missing people from further abroad than our county," Blade informed me before waving his enforcers over. "Call this in, get a team out here. I want everyone and everything in this area catalogued. We need to increase the patrols, too. Teams of four or more, no less, at least one with an affinity for light."

They nodded and began barking orders while my mates ushered me back towards the house.

The rest of the evening was a bustle of activity, with people in and out from all three packs, the local coven, and even the Elder's Council.

I was exhausted and saddened by the events of the day, and more than ready to put an end to Oberon, once and for all.

*

Over the next few days, we received a flurry of new information, which helped us piece together much of the puzzle that we had been struggling with. What we learned brought me hope as well as a healthy dose of rage. Oberon had been active in regions throughout the world. He was abducting people from every supernatural branch, only those with an affinity for potent light magic had escaped his clutches, not for his lack of trying. We had reports from nephilim, light witches, and other fae clans with affinities similar to my Moon Clan ancestors that spoke of shadows trying to invade them, but their native magic burning them out.

Oberon was careful, not showing his face to any of those who might be able to resist his shadows, which had allowed him to walk about normally during the day as just another fae. Now that we knew his face, Glenn and Blade had disseminated information about the disowned king. He wouldn't be able to continue moonlighting as just another powerful supernatural.

Of course, we were worried that losing that avenue of attack might make him desperate, potentially driving him to move his plans up. Whatever they were. Even with Orin, and now Titania's, help, we had no clue what Oberon's endgame was. Once upon a time, it was to protect his people, but Orin had little hope of that being the actual goal now, and I was inclined to agree with him.

We were beginning to formulate a plan of how to put a stop to the Darkness and Oberon once and for all, but we were still missing some of the pieces. I was worried about that cavern. Blade was trying, but he couldn't find any useful information about how it might tie into the

Darkness, or how exactly Oberon was using it to manipulate people. I knew it was at the center of everything, though, I just didn't know how yet.

I was once again left with more questions than answers, but as I looked around at the three strong, fierce mates by my side, I knew that between us, we would figure everything out, one way or another.

I was here, and they were here, and we *would* find a way to rescue Camille and the others. Together.

Printed in Great Britain
by Amazon